MICHAEL SANTINO

The Frontline: Season 1 Episode 1

Pilot Episode

Preface

You're about to begin reading the first episode of a serial. It's written in short installments that are meant to be read in order and you're starting in the right place. Each episode is designed to be read in about two hours or so. I know it's out of the ordinary to call the installments episodes, but I like to march to my own beat. You can get all the episodes individually or get the complete first season (episodes 1-7 packaged together at a discount) on Amazon or your Kindle.

If you enjoy your visit, go to kolecounty.com to sign up for my email list and get some free bonus content. If you have any questions, you can email me at michaelsantino@protonmail.com.

With that said, the story begins on Monday, September 11th, 2017, in Kole County.

1

Chapter 1

Brooke Littman was sitting at her desk reading an article by Sonia Gonzales in the *Daily Freeman*. Approaching sixty years old, she was set in her ways and not about to start getting her news from the internet. But stubbornness didn't come with age for her. It was baked in from go.

She was an Assistant District Attorney in Kole County, but for all intents and purposes, and if you asked any of the other ADAs, she ran the office. Over the years, she had built deep trust with her boss, Kole County District Attorney Ron Peters, who was on the back nine of his career, probably logging half the hours he used to, and even that would be generous.

Ron hadn't lost his passion and still had some spark, but at seventy-six, he was ready to ride into the sunset. It was only his sense of loyalty to his friends in the Democratic Party who implored him to run for reelection every two years and to his ADAs like Brooke that he kept it going. If he were to retire, the Republicans would take over the office as no Democrat besides Ron had won a countywide race in Kole since before Obama was elected. Brooke and the other ADAs knew that and happily picked up his slack. It was in everyone's interest to do so.

Brooke considered herself tough but fair, and all of her colleagues agreed with the former. Seeing to it that criminals found their way into cages was what she was passionate about. She had prosecutor blood running through her veins and probably would do the job for free if Kole County didn't insist on paying her.

"Brooke, you've got a call on line two," the office secretary's voice came over the intercom. Brooke took a sip of coffee, put down the *Freeman*, and picked up the phone.

"Hello, Miss Littman, thank you for taking my call," the voice said.

"No problem. Who is this, and how can I help you?"

"My name's not important. I'm calling because I have information on the American Dawn case, and I want you to have it."

"Well, let's have it then," she said.

"Not over the phone. In-person," he replied.

"The case is nearly closed. There's a plea deal on the table, and they're going to take it."

"If you knew what I know and have what I have, you would retract the plea offer, Miss Littman."

"What do you have, sir?"

"I have recordings."

"How did you get these recordings?"

"I took them myself at American Dawn's meetings. This could save hundreds of lives, Miss Littman."

"Okay, you've got my attention. What time can you come in?"

"Not at your office. I'll meet you at Nellie's Soul Kitchen on Main at four this afternoon. Sit alone in a booth. I'll come in and order a coffee from the counter. While it's being prepared, I'll walk back to the bathroom and drop an envelope on your table. Don't acknowledge me. Take the envelope and put it in your bag quickly. I'll contact you tomorrow in case you have any questions."

"Fair enough. I'll be there," Brooke said before hanging up the phone. She immediately picked it back up and dialed the secretary.

"Nancy, tell Bobby and Kate I need to see them immediately."

Stevenson and Roseline Pierre were both the children of immigrants from Haiti, and both arrived here when they were young, shortly before the refugee crisis in 1991. Roseline was a home health aide, and Stevenson, a lineman for the phone company. Stevenson put in for a transfer with the phone company from the city and moved the family to Kole County, where his salary would go a lot farther, and they could actually afford to own a modest home. After a few years, Roseline always regretted the move. She preferred to be closer to her family, friends, and community. Roseline felt out of place in Kole, as if her neighbors, or at least some of them, would prefer she go back to where she came from. That feeling was increasing with each passing year.

Stevenson had an outgoing, very sunny disposition and could feel comfortable in any room or with any group of people. He liked living in Kole, but he would have liked living anywhere because his life really revolved around Rosaline and their seven-year-old son James. Home for Stevenson was wherever he was with them. This morning that happened to be at his kitchen table.

"What are you going to learn in school today, son?" Stevenson asked.

"I don't know. I haven't gone yet," James replied.

"Of course not. But what are they teaching you this week?"

"They are teaching me about vowels," James said. Roseline smiled as he struggled to pronounce the word.

"Where are you going to be working today, Stevenson?" she asked.

"I'll be downtown mostly."

"I need to go grocery shopping, but I can't today. Can you bring home dinner?" Roseline asked.

"Sure. Where do you want me to pick up from?" Stevenson asked.

"If you're downtown, then definitely Nellie's Soul Kitchen."

"I get off at four, so I'll stop there and be back here by about five," Stevenson said as he got up from the table and kissed them both before walking out the door.

Jerry Ramos was sitting alone at a table in the back corner of Fin's, focused intently on his phone while nursing a Coors. The bar was empty. It was too late for the lunch crowd yet still a little early for happy hour. Jerry had a scowl on his face, or at least it appeared that way. That was just the way his face looked.

He was in his late thirties but looked older. The semi-permanent scowl resulted in people keeping their distance from him for the most part, which was all for the better because he was a nasty son of a bitch. Jerry was waiting for his brother Matthew Ramos, who was supposed to meet him for a drink before an appointment they had. Matthew was late, but that was fine because Jerry preferred to drink alone anyway.

Together they were known locally as the Conejo brothers.

When they were young, they'd get ripped on by other kids as their last name didn't match their white skin tone. They were also pretty fast, faster than the other kids. Somewhere along the way, they got dubbed the Conejo brothers, as in Spanish for rabbit.

Matthew walked into Fin's and headed directly to the bar to say hello to Kevin Finnerty, the owner. "What can I get for you?" Fin asked.

"I'm afraid this is a quick visit. I'm late. Jerry and I have business to attend to," Matthew replied.

"You *are* late," Jerry growled from across the room. "You like to keep me waiting like your time is more valuable than mine. Where are we meeting our man?" Jerry asked.

"Across the street at Nellie's Soul Kitchen. We should get going. He said we needed to be there exactly at four."

Brooke Littman arrived at Nellie's about five minutes before 4 p.m. She pulled her Wrangler into the parking lot, gathered her things, and checked her look in the mirror. She was striking, not just for a fifty-nine-year-old, but period.

Nellie's Soul Kitchen was previously a run-of-the-mill diner and had that look. Brooke carried her briefcase up the stairs into the vestibule, passing the empty space where the cigarette machine used to be. She didn't wait to be seated in the empty restaurant and took one of the booths along the front windows. Hearing the little bell on the front door ring as it closed, a young man came out from the kitchen. Brooke looked up at him and judged him to be in his late twenties. He was black, thin, and clean-shaven.

"I'll be with you in just a moment. I'm the only one working today," he said before disappearing back into the kitchen.

Brooke pulled her phone out and began dividing her attention between her email and watching the parking lot as she waited. A few minutes later, the Conejo brothers crossed the street from Fin's Bar and entered Nellie's, triggering the bell to ring again. They took seats at the counter. Matthew swiveled his stool back to face Brooke. "No one seems to be minding the store. Are we alone here?" he asked her.

"There's a guy in the kitchen. He's the only one working," Brooke replied as the man in the kitchen came out to take her order, signaling to the Conejo brothers he'd be with them in a minute.

"I'll just take a diet coke and your soup of the day," she said before he could ask.

As he walked back towards the counter, Brooke heard one of the men ask, "So, do you have anything for us, Jermaine?" but before he could answer, the bell rang again. Stevenson Pierre walked in.

Jermaine looked at him and said, "Sir, I'm the only one here, so it'll be a few minutes."

"No problem. I can wait," Stevenson said.

Jermaine looked back at Matthew and Jerry and said, "Give me a minute," before heading back into the kitchen and out of sight. Brooke kept her eyes on the parking lot, but there was no sign of anyone approaching the restaurant. The Conejos sat waiting impatiently while Stevenson sat smiling, reading something on his phone. Thirty seconds passed before the restaurant was blown to hell by a blast that left a raging fire, scattered piles of burning debris, and body parts in the spot where Nellie's Soul Kitchen used to be.

2

Chapter 2

The Assistant Special Agent in Charge at the Winthrop Field Office of the FBI was Jackie Davis. Jackie was beginning to serve his final year as ASAC, with his retirement scheduled to happen the day of his tenth anniversary in the position. When you looked at him, retirement wouldn't come to mind. He was an avid runner, still logging a few miles each morning before reporting for duty. If you didn't know better, you'd think he was mid-career and climbing, but he was about to hit the FBI's mandatory retirement age.

Jackie was at peace with it, having grandchildren to play with, a good pension, and more than enough claims to fame within the annals of FBI lore. He'd been a lead investigator on the case that took down the Aryan Republican Army, a domestic terrorist group that arose in response to the Feds' handling of Waco and Ruby Ridge. Also known as the Midwest Bank Bandits, they robbed banks to fund their activities. Jackie led the pursuit that resulted in the arrest of their ringleader.

This afternoon, Jackie was sitting with Special Agent Christopher Odacio, who was briefing him on a case. He had taken a liking to Odacio years ago and had taken him under his wing. In official settings with superiors and reports, he referred to him as Agent Odacio, but in most settings, he called him "Scout," as in Boy Scout. Their conversation was interrupted when Jackie's phone rang.

"Excuse me one moment," Jackie said as he picked up the receiver. "This is ASAC Davis."

Odacio pulled out his cell phone and went to ESPN.com while he waited.

"Where?" Jackie said with a strain in his voice that caught Odacio's attention. "How many?"

"What was that, sir? What's wrong?"

"There was an explosion at a restaurant in Kole. The whole building is blown out."

"How many casualties?"

"They don't know yet. It just happened."

"What do they think?"

"They think it was a bomb, Scout."

"You know I live in Kole, sir."

"Clear your schedule. The name of the place is Nellie's Soul Kitchen."

"I know the place."

"Call me as soon as you have a read on the situation."

"Yessir." Special Agent Odacio grabbed his coat and made a beeline to his Cherokee in the parking garage. He checked the mirrors and peeled out, heading for the interstate. He dialed his wife Kristen by voice command.

"Hi." her voice came over the car speakers.

"I'm going to be late. Did you hear what happened?"

"No. I'm still at work. What's up?" she asked.

"Remember that place we stopped at for lunch when I took

you to DMV?"

"Yeah… the soul food place on Main. I like that place. What about it?" she asked.

"Nellie's Soul Kitchen. It blew up."

"What do you mean it blew up?"

"Like a bomb. It blew up," he said.

"Jesus. Are they okay?"

"The people in the place? No. Not at all. They're dead. Well, I think they're dead."

"How many?" she asked.

"I don't know anything yet. I just know it blew up, and they think it was a bomb. I'm heading there now."

"What the fuck? Who blows up a luncheonette?" she asked, exasperated.

"I don't know. It's the first time I've come across it."

"Hmm. I wonder…" she paused.

"What?"

"I don't know. It's a black-owned business. Do you think…"

"I hadn't considered that. I haven't considered anything yet. I'm on the interstate heading there now."

"Ok. Be careful. What time do you think…" she began to ask.

"I don't know. This could take a while. Eat without me. Can you give Frank his meds?" Frank was their lab.

"Yeah. What does he get?"

"Just a tablespoon mixed in with the wet food. It goes right through him. Feed him when you are ready to go on a walk," he said.

"I'll take him with me on a run. He's getting fat; he can use the exercise."

"He's fine."

"No. He's getting fat. Have you seen him lately? Oh, by the

way, your mother called right after you left this morning," she said.

"What did she want?"

"To talk. Chewed my ear off for about twenty minutes,"

"What about?"

"I don't know. Something about the people who cut her lawn, they're doing it wrong; she doesn't like the cut of their jib."

"What does that mean?" Odacio asked.

"I don't know. You should call her. She seemed lonely. Like it was all a pretext to get you over there to cut her grass without asking you. Kind of sweet in a way, but in her way."

"And what way is that?"

"You know, 'illegal immigrants this, illegal immigrants that… I miss my son and want him to visit me.'"

"Fine. I'll call her."

"Don't forget we have to go to Jack and Donna's on Saturday. They want to do a game night," Kristen said.

"Okay, sounds good."

"I should get back to work. Love you."

"Love you too," he said before hanging up the phone.

Christopher Odacio wasn't born and raised in Kole, but he and Kristen bought their house there when he got assigned to the FBI field office in Winthrop, which was just forty miles north of the Kole County Line. You could still get an old house on a nice property for under $150,000 in Kole, and its mix of farmland and patchwork of small towns held a lot of charm.

Christopher excelled at sports as a kid and worked as a lifeguard in the summers. On more than one occasion, he probably prevented a child from drowning and found a rush in the heroism thing. He thrived in the military-like environment that his former drill sergeant-turned football coach provided for four years of high school. Encouraged by his coach, Christopher enlisted in the Army, spending a few years stationed in Germany. He considered making a career of it but took the free ride to college on the GI Bill and ultimately landed himself in the FBI, which was proving to be a good fit.

Christopher was smart, but Kristen was smarter. And they both knew it. Christopher always thought that she would make a great FBI agent or detective. Really a great anything, because she was good at everything. Her mother passed when she was young, and her father didn't have steady work. His house painting business failed when he took a bad fall and got addicted to painkillers long before any public awareness of the coming opioid crisis. Born into different circumstances, Kristen might have found her way to a top college and high-powered profession, but she enjoyed being a nurse.

Christopher came from a more stable, middle-class family and benefited from many of the advantages and breaks that most middle-class kids enjoy, even if they don't realize it. His relationship with Kristen made him realize it. He always worked as hard, or even a little harder, than the next guy, and he was smart, maybe even a little smarter than the next guy, but he wasn't exceptional. He thought Kristen was exceptional. Between marrying her and getting into the FBI, most days he felt like he'd hit the jackpot.

As he approached the interstate exit for downtown Kole, his phone rang. "This is Special Agent Odacio."

"Hold for ASAC Davis," a woman's voice said. About ten seconds passed.

"Scout, it's ASAC."

"I know, sir. Your secretary told me to hold for you when she dialed."

11

"There's a survivor. He got his eggs scrambled, but he's alive," Jackie said.

"Is he at the scene?"

"He's at the Kole County Medical Center."

"Got it. I've got to pass Nellie's to get to the Medical Center. I'll make a quick stop, then go to KCMC."

"That's fine. There's a local cop named Bonner. It's his crime scene," Jackie said.

"Local cop? It's gotta be a state trooper. The local police force was disbanded about five years ago. I remember it was one of those nasty local fights. I think the chief at the time ended up eating his gun after it was all over. The county contracts with the state police now."

"In any case, his name is Bonner. He knows you're coming."

"Sir, I've been to Nellie's. It's a soul food place."

"And?"

"Why do you think someone would blow up a soul food joint?"

"That's what you're there to figure out, Scout."

"Yeah, but I wonder whether it was targeted because it was a black-owned business."

ASAC Davis paused. "Could be. We're seeing a lot more of that kind of activity these days. People seem to think it's a Trump effect. I think it's more about the reaction to Obama. That election awoke something dark in this country. Regardless, keep an open mind, and follow the facts."

12

3

Chapter 3

Special Agent Odacio got about three blocks from the site of Nellie's and parked as the area was taped off and guarded by state troopers. He showed his credentials and passed the first checkpoint. Downtown looked different than he'd imagined. In his mind, it was a war zone, but Main St was pretty empty and looked unusually peaceful, if anything.

As he got closer, the debris where Nellie's used to be was scattered all over the parking lot, and the smell of burning tar, rubber, and something else hung in the air. Nellie's had sat set back from the street with its own parking lot, which was good because it meant that the damage was localized. The surrounding buildings, which were storefronts on the street level and apartments upstairs, were unscathed.

Odacio stepped over the sign that must have hung over the doorway just hours ago to speak to a state trooper guarding the scene. He flashed his credentials and said he was looking for Bonner. The trooper pointed him out, but he didn't need to. Bonner was clearly in command, taller than the other officers and directing in his demeanor. To Odacio, Bonner looked old and weathered, but like a survivor. He looked like the kind of guy you could shoot three times and assume he'd survive somehow. The kind of guy you might have cast Clint Eastwood to play about twenty years ago.

Bonner quickly made eye contact with Odacio but just as quickly looked away, as if he had seen everything he needed to. Odacio approached him and pulled his credentials from his breast pocket.

"You can put that away, son. I saw you coming; I know who you are," Bonner said.

"Good to meet you, sir. I'm Special Agent Odacio."

"Yeah, I just told you I know who you are. I'm Senior Investigator Bonner"

"Good to meet you…" As Odacio raised his hand to shake, Bonner looked away, so he didn't see it, or so as not to see it. Odacio wasn't sure and put his hand back at his side. "What do we know?"

"We'll know more shortly. We've got one survivor. One of the workers, I think. He's at KCMC, but he's fine. Our boys are canvassing the neighborhood, been out there about forty minutes. We know there is more than one dead in there, but the bodies are all blown apart. Could be five, could be seven, could be less. Can't tell yet."

"Any witnesses?"

"No."

"What do you think, sir?"

"I don't think anything yet. Don't know enough." Bonner barked.

"This was a black-owned business. Do you think it might have been racially motivated?" Odacio asked.

"The hammer sure sees a lot of nails, doesn't it? You're not from around here, are you?"

"I live five miles up Creekside Rd."

"I didn't ask you where you lived. I asked you where you were from."

"Sir, maybe we got off on the wrong foot. I'm Christopher Odacio. I live in town, I'm with the FBI, and I'm here to help."

"Well, Christopher Odacio, I appreciate it. I'm Brett Bonner. Hopefully, we can find our way together."

"Brett Bonner. That's got a good ring to it," Odacio said, trying to stick out an olive branch.

"Christopher Odacio, what kind of name is that?" Bonner responded.

"Sir?"

"What kind of name is that, son? Where are your people from?"

"My mother is mostly Italian, and my father was Cuban, I think."

"You think?"

"I don't think much of it at all. I think I'm American, sir."

"Ok, you'll ride with me to KCMC. Let's go see if that boy has come to yet."

Bonner and Odacio didn't talk on the ride. Wichita Lineman came on the radio. Bonner said he liked Glen Campbell, but Odacio took it as Bonner's way of saying he didn't want to talk, or more accurately, hear Odacaio talk. They pulled into KCMC and found their way to the room where the survivor was. As they were walking in, Bonner said, "the kid's name is Jermaine."

Odacio pulled out his credentials, but Bonner didn't bother. Jermaine had a cartoon-style lump on the left side of his forehead and some bandages below his eye covering up a cut or scrape and one on his right hand. Odacio began before Bonner, "We need to ask you some questions, Jermaine. Are you up to it?"

"Yeah."

"You work at Nellie's?" Odacio took the lead.

"I did."

"You a cook? A waiter?" Bonner interjected.

"I run the place," Jermaine said.

"Are you the owner?" Bonner continued.

"I didn't say I own it. I said I run the place. Nellie is my mother. She owns it."

"Was she in there, Jermaine?" Odacio asked.

"No. She hasn't been in there in quite some time. She got hit by a car about a year back. Broke her hip and leg. I was running the place temporarily, but the recovery has been really slow. She's always in pain."

"I'm sorry to hear that but glad to know she wasn't in there," Odacio said.

"Me too. Do you know who did this to us?"

"No. But we want to find out, and we need your help. We need to know everything you remember," Odacio said.

"How many people were in the restaurant?" Bonner asked.

"Four, I think. There was a white woman, maybe forty-five or fifty years old, and a black guy with an accent, like a Caribbean accent. I think he was in his thirties. And two white guys who came in together, I'd say they were in their thirties as well."

"Were you the only one working?" Bonner asked.

"I was the only one today. I usually work the front, but the cook called out."

"What were you doing out back when the bomb went off?"

Bonner asked.

"I went out to smoke a cigarette."

"You got four customers waiting, you're all alone, and you went for a cigarette?" Bonner asked.

"Yeah."

"That's how you run the place?" Bonner asked.

"You know, I didn't ask for this. I'm doing it so that she don't lose the restaurant,"

"Let's get back to the moment right before you went for a cigarette," Odacio redirected. "The customers, did any of them look suspicious? Were they carrying bags?"

"Man, the woman had a briefcase. Looked professional. It didn't look like she was carrying a bomb. The three men, I didn't really notice what they were wearing or what they were carrying. I remember one of the white ones was ugly looking. But I didn't see no bomb."

"What about earlier in the day, other customers? Did anyone look suspicious?" Odacio asked.

"Honestly, it was a normal day. It was a normal crowd. Some people I recognize come in often; some of them I ain't never seen before. But that's normal. It's all a little blurry. I don't know if it's cause I hit my head or that I was mostly in the back cooking. I didn't get a good look at people, and I definitely didn't have time to chat,"

"Alright, let's try something else here. Do you or your mother have any enemies? Anyone you have done wrong, who might want to get you?" Bonner asked.

"No. I keep to myself. I don't fuck with no one's girlfriends. I'm not into drugs. Mama, no one wants to get her, and if they did, they would have done so already. Most of the time, I'm at the restaurant, till now that is."

"What about insurance, Jermaine? Is the place insured?" Bonner barked.

"Shit. I hope so. That might be one silver lining. Come to think of it, I did pay a bill to Allstate or one of them some months back."

"What's the policy worth?" Bonner asked, Odacio noticing his fist clenched.

"Fuck if I know. I just told you I paid a bill, that's what I remember. I hope it's insured for a million dollars. But I don't fucking know. And don't think I don't know what you're getting at. Fucking bomb my mama's restaurant? Fuck you."

Before Bonner responded, Odacio cut in. "Let's all take it down a notch. We'll need that policy when you get out of here, Jermaine. Do you remember how long you were outside before the explosion?"

"Couldn't have been a minute. I'm pretty lucky, I guess."

"I'd say you are *very* lucky, Jermaine. I want to take you to Vegas with me," Bonner said.

"Man, I get it; you're doing the good cop bad cop routine. You two practice this shit, or you improvise it?"

"We just met," Odacio said. "Give us something to go on, Jermaine. Anything, any little detail that seemed out of place? Did anything look off to you?"

"I really wish I had something to give you, officer. But I don't." He paused a moment. "The only thing I can think of, and this probably ain't anything; the woman kept on looking out the window like she was waiting on someone. That was just the impression that I got. If I can think of anything else, maybe when this concussion wears off, I'll tell you. I want you to find the sons of bitches who did this, and I want them to fry."

"Bitches, Jermaine? Them? You just said 'them.' Why is it

18

more than one person? Who are they?" Bonner pounced.

"Jesus man, they, them, him? It's a fucking figure of speech!"

"I think we have what we need for tonight," Odacio said. They stepped out and closed the door behind them.

In the elevator, Bonner growled, "That son of a bitch is lying! He's hiding something. I can smell it on him."

"Slow down. Don't you think you're jumping the gun?" Odacio asked.

"He wasn't giving it to us straight. Don't tell me you buy that lucky cigarette bit. And he was acting odd."

"You mean the way one might act if they just almost died and were getting accused of a capital crime? Let's think about this for a second. Where was he found? Ten, maybe fifteen feet from the building? You're telling me the kid plants a bomb in his own restaurant and only puts 10 feet of distance between him and the blast? It makes no sense." Odacio asserted.

"I tell you, that boy knows something he ain't telling us. I know guilt when I see it, and he was covered in it head to toe."

"He was covered in it head to toe? What are you saying?"

"Oh, don't start that shit with me, boy. I don't give a fuck that he's black," Bonner said.

"I didn't say anything."

"Fuck you. You didn't have to say it. I saw it on your face. Don't think your Ivy League smarts are too much for me to see through."

"I went to a state school," Odacio retorted. "Can you calm the fuck down?"

Before he had a chance to oblige, a text alert went off on Bonner's cell. He scanned the screen.

"We got leads on two of the victims," Bonner began. "Someone in the District Attorney's office didn't return to work after a trip to Nellie's, and there's a frantic woman who believes her husband was there. Let's divide and conquer. We can use some time apart."

"Which do you want?" Odacio asked.

"What's that saying about dead lawyers at the bottom of the sea? I'll take the hysterical woman. You head over to the District Attorney's office. And I'm gonna get a man on Jermaine. I don't want him up and skipping town on account I put a scare into him. I'll drop you at your car."

4

Chapter 4

Agent Odacio hopped into his Cherokee, pulled out of his spot, and headed towards the DA's office. It was also downtown and only about a three-minute drive. As he drove, he replayed the conversation with Jermaine in his mind, trying to see what Bonner saw, giving Bonner the benefit of the doubt. But Jermaine seemed straight up to Odacio, like a kid who just went through a traumatic experience. Odacio had caught Jermaine's reference to 'them' as well and made a mental note of it, but them *is* a figure of speech. Also, it *would* be reasonable to assume that more than one person was involved in a bombing.

Agent Odacio entered the office, where three people were waiting for him. At least two of the three had been crying but seemed to have just pulled themselves together. He recognized one of them immediately, and that's who greeted him. "Hello, I'm Ron Peters."

"Yes, I recognize you from your mail. I think I voted for you," Odacio said. "I'm Special Agent Odacio, Federal Bureau of Investigation."

Peters motioned to decline the credentials. "This is Bobby Sokolov and Kate Peters," he said as they each extended a hand.

Odacio shook Bobby's hand and then moved onto Kate. He glanced at the District Attorney and back at Kate. "And you're you his daughter?"

"No," she replied with a smile. "We get that all the time. Just a coincidence with a common last name."

"I almost didn't hire her, afraid someone would charge me with nepotism, but Brooke convinced me otherwise," Ron said. They both looked at each other, and Kate teared up.

"We don't know who was or wasn't in there. It's not definitely the case that…" Odacio started.

"No. It is definitely the case," Ron began. "No, if's, and's, or but's about it. Brooke worked until 7 p.m. on a light day. She told them both she was coming back to debrief her meeting," he said, pointing to Kate and Bobby. "There's no way on God's green earth that that woman forgot or decided to do something else. She was in there, and she's in a better place now."

"She was going there to meet someone?" Odacio asked, remembering what Jermaine had said.

"Yes. We got an anonymous call," Kate said.

"Please, tell me about it," Odacio replied.

"Are you following the American Dawn case?" she asked.

"No, but it sounds familiar."

"Okay, we'll brief you on that. But long story short, we were about to plea out a charge on a hate crime any day now. Brooke got a call this morning…"

"What time?" Odacio asked.

"About 9 a.m. The person said they were a defector from American Dawn and that they had recorded their meetings. They claimed American Dawn was planning something horrific and that hundreds of people could die if it wasn't prevented," Kate said.

"What else?"

"Well, not much else. He wouldn't give his name, and he wouldn't come here. He said he would only meet in public," Kate said.

"Did Brooke suggest the location and time, or did the caller?" Odacio asked.

"I don't know. I think he said the time, and she said the place?" Kate said, looking at Bobby in case he remembered.

"I don't remember her saying that, Kate," Bobby chimed in.

"Were either of you present when the call came in?"

"We were present as in we were here, but we weren't in her office. She called us in right after she got off the call," Kate said.

"This is very important. I need you to think back to that conversation when she briefed you, really think. Did she suggest the location, or did the caller choose the location?"

"I can't say I remember for certain. I'm don't think she said one way or the other," Bobby said.

"I don't know for sure either. I think I remember her saying that he said it needed to be in public and that it had to be today. But I don't know," Kate added.

"Okay, but what about Nellie's? Was that a place Brooke liked to go or schedule meetings at? Does she like soul food?"

"I mean, on one hand," Kate began, "Brooke liked all different ethnic foods. She was one of those types who could just eat and eat and eat and never gained a pound. On the other hand, I don't remember her ever doing a meeting previously at Nellie's. It's close to here, but other places are closer."

"I don't know," Bobby said, "but I doubt that Brooke would pick Nellie's. Not because of the food, but because it's, or it was, kind of small. There's not a lot of privacy. But then again, it sounded like more of a handoff of the recordings than a meeting."

"Well, maybe Nellie's is a good spot," Ron began. "If you're a white supremacist who doesn't want to be seen by other white supremacists, a black-owned soul food restaurant downtown might be as good a spot as any."

"That's a good point. Ok, tell me about American Dawn," Odacio said

"I'll get the case file," Kate said as she got out of her chair and headed to another room.

"I take it American Dawn was Brooke's case?" Odacio asked.

"On some level, every case was Brooke's case. She was one of the sharpest attorneys, hell, one of the sharpest people I ever met. But yeah, this one was definitely her's," Ron said.

"Tell me about the case,"

"We were vaguely aware of the existence of American Dawn for a while. Not by the name, though. It was the local paper that came up with that. At first, it seemed mostly like a social club. From what we understand, it started with some guys getting together and going hunting but has since escalated into something approaching an informal militia group," Ron said.

"How many people are involved?" Odacio asked.

"They claim to have 50 members in some online posts," Bobby began. "I'd say there's a core of 20 people. It revolved around Keith Brown, his son, who's also named Keith but goes by Junior, and Brody Wilcox, Keith's friend. Others come and go; some just come for the hunting, others really buy into their right-wing bullshit. They meet on the third Saturday of the month in Keith's barn."

Kate returned, took a seat, and handed a file to Odacio.

"You can keep that copy," she said.

"Thanks. Does American Dawn have a stated purpose?" Odacio asked.

"Defending freedom and liberty. They say. It's really a toxic mix of nationalists, racists, and QANON followers. You know the people who think Hillary Clinton runs a child sex trafficking ring?" Bobby said.

"I am familiar. What was American Dawn's run-in with the law?" Odacio asked.

"Well, it was Brody. He was driving home one night on Lake drive. He saw two cars parked on the side of the road. He pulled his truck over and ended up shooting both drivers. One died, the other survived. There was Tim Raines. Young black guy. He survived a shot to the abdomen. The other guy, Vance Parker, took one to the skull, didn't make it."

"Was Vance black as well?" Odacio asked.

"Light brown skin, mixed-race, I think," Bobby said.

"What led to the shooting?" Odacio asked.

"It depends on who you believe. At first, Brody said the two men were suspicious. In later statements, he said he thought they were broken down and wanted to help. Raines said words were exchanged, and the situation escalated quickly. Brody drew his gun, and then Vance pulled a knife. Brody says it was the other way around. Whatever anyone says, those men wouldn't have been shot if they were white," Bobby said.

"Where is Raines now?" Odacio asked.

"Locked up. He was on parole at the time of the incident, and they found opioids in his vehicle, a lot of opioids. That was a violation, obviously. Brooke had a case pending against him on opioid sales," Bobby said. "I'm surprised you haven't heard about this. It was all over the news in February and March.

Everyone was talking about it."

"My stepfather passed around that time. I was out of town helping my mother sell the house and move into something smaller. I wasn't following the local news in Kole," Odacio said.

"Alright. Well, this case and the attention it got made American Dawn a thing. Everyone had a field day with it. Keith tried to make Brody into a martyr. Like he was some political prisoner. They raised over a million dollars in small donations to their GoFundMe or whatever it was. Suddenly, this small group of racist losers had a full-fledged, funded organization on their hands. And if we're to believe that man who called Brooke, maybe a domestic terrorist organization," Bobby said.

"Where did the name come from?" Odacio asked.

"Junior. There was a little gathering, like a rally outside the county jail to support Brody. Junior was interviewed on News12. He went on some rant. Said something like 'We're not going to be replaced. We need a new American dawn in this country,' and the media just ran with it. Then they started calling themselves American Dawn, put up a website. You know how it goes," Ron said.

"Okay. I'm going to read this file. I'll have follow-up questions. I assume you have an emergency contact for Brooke?" Odacio asked.

"I already made that call," Ron said.

Agent Odacio got back in his Cherokee. He put the key in the ignition, then realized he didn't know where he was headed. He paused for a moment and decided to call Kristen.

"Hey. How you doing?" Kristen asked.

"You know, a little worn. What about you?"

"I'm hungry. I don't want to cook just for me. I was thinking of running out to Enzo's or Mickie D's."

"Yeah, me too," he said.

"You're going to McDonald's too?" she asked, surprised.

"No. Me too, as in I'm hungry."

"Where are you?"

"In the Jeep. Heading back to the scene."

"Is anything open down there?" Kristen asked.

"The bar across the street. They have burgers and stuff."

"You want company?"

"I'm still working on this," Odacio said.

"Yeah, but you're going to stop and eat. Do you want company?"

He hesitated for a second and then, "Definitely. You'll need to park a few blocks away."

"What's the name of the place?"

"I don't know. It's the bar that's open across the street from a war zone. You can't miss it," Odacio said.

"Gotcha. See you in ten minutes."

Odacio put the car in drive and started towards Main St. He thought about calling Bonner to brief him but realized that they forgot to exchange numbers or business cards in the midst of all the pleasantries. Then he remembered he owed Jackie a call, so he dialed him instead.

"What do we know, Scout?" Jackie answered, skipping the hello.

"The survivor is Jermaine Childs. He's Nellie's son and has been minding the shop for the last year since she was in an accident. He was the only person working. Stepped outside for a smoke and kaboom. We think there were four victims inside. Not certain of that, though. It's a weird one, sir."

"How so?"

"I just left the DA's office. One of the victims was an Assistant District Attorney, Brooke Littman. She got an anonymous call this morning, goes to meet the caller at Nellie's at four p.m. A few minutes later, the place explodes."

"She was lured there?" Jackie asked.

"Unclear. She might have picked the spot. She briefed a couple of the ADAs on it, but neither of them can remember her explicitly saying if the meeting spot was her idea or the anonymous caller's."

"What's the context of the call?"

"American Dawn. They…"

"I'm familiar with them."

"Well, someone called up claiming to be a defector who had taped the meetings. Said they were planning something nasty and that hundreds of people would die if they weren't stopped," Odacio said.

"I don't think they're all that much. I've been monitoring them. More like a bunch of blowhards with rifles who like to play soldier on Saturdays. They're not a terrorist organization," Jackie said.

"It could be they've evolved, sir. They may be graduating. You've been monitoring them? Who's assigned to it?"

"Not like that. They're in our backyard. I read about it in the news. I get alerts on them, joined their list. I follow them on Twitter and such."

"This ADA, Littman, was the lead prosecutor on the case involving one of their leaders, Brody something. It seems like she was targeted, sir."

"Why not shoot her in the head walking from her car to her front door. Bombing a restaurant seems like a blunt approach, no?"

"I don't know. Black business. ADA prosecutor on their case. Seems like two for the price of one."

"That could be coincidental," Jackie said.

"Pretty long odds on this being a coincidence, wouldn't you say?"

"Just the black business part. What about that caller, the defector. Any thoughts there?"

"Yes. Obviously, it could be legit, exactly what it looks like. Or, it could also be one of the higher-ups at American Dawn posing as a defector to lure her to a specific place at a specific time," Odacio posited.

"We'll pull the phone records to try and get a lead on the call source, but don't get your hopes up. Anyone with half a brain would have used a burner phone."

"Hmm," Odacio said.

"What are you thinking, Scout?"

"There were four victims we know of from Jermaine. The two white guys, who came in together, we don't know who they are yet. But I hadn't considered that one of them could have been the anonymous caller. I guess I was thinking of the anonymous caller as one person, but he could have easily come with someone else," Odacio said.

"The call was bait for a trap, or it was legit. If it were bait, he or his partner wouldn't have been at the scene. If it was legit, it's likely the caller would have mentioned that he would be coming with someone when he called the ADA." Jackie said.

"Maybe American Dawn was a step ahead of them, or they thought one thing was happening, and they were getting double-crossed," Odacio said.

"That seems like a stretch," Jackie said. "I'm skeptical of the American Dawn theory. I think they're more likely a smokescreen. They're not a terrorist organization. However, if it was them, then the most plausible explanation is that the call was merely a lure to put the ADA in the right place at the right time. Did you connect with Bonner?" Jackie asked.

"Yeah, he's a fucking delight. We split up before the meeting at the DA's office. He's hot for Jermaine as the perp, the guy running Nellie's. I thought the kid was fine," Odacio said.

"We should work up a full dossier on him. Just to be safe," Jackie said.

"I'm sure Bonner has got the entire troop on that, sir."

"Nonetheless, we'll look into it."

"I'll send over the names of the American Dawn ringleaders as well. Keith Brown and Keith Brown Junior are definitely on the list to start, but I haven't had a chance to read the full file. I'm going to eat and then do that next."

"Ok, stay in communication."

"Yessir."

5

Chapter 5

O dacio parked and made his way to Fin's, noticing that Kristen had already arrived. When he walked in, the place was crowded. Kristen was seated with her back to the door. She knew Christopher didn't like to sit with his back facing the door. As he walked over, she got up and gave him a big hug, squeezing hard. He sat.

"You didn't order yet, right?" he asked.

"Just a beer. Are you having one?"

"No. Probably just a soda," he said as he looked down at the menu printed under the glass that covered the table. It was standard bar fare. The bartender came out from behind the bar and asked if they wanted drinks to start.

"A Pepsi and a glass of water with ice would be great."

"Do you need more time for food?"

"Yes, just a couple of minutes," Kristen said.

"It's been a long day."

"Can you talk about it?" Kristen asked.

"I shouldn't. Did you remember Frank's meds?"

"Yeah. I said I would do it. I took him on the run too. He

couldn't keep up with me, had to cut it short."

"You're full of it," Odacio said.

"No. I'm telling you. He's too fat."

"I know you're telling me he's too fat. You're adding in a lie to make your point," Odacio said.

"You don't know when I'm lying."

"I definitely know when you're lying," Odacio retorted.

"Do not."

"Do too."

"Okay. Let's put it to a test. Let's play two truths and a lie," she said, smiling and giving him a look like I'm gonna kick your butt.

"How does it work?"

"Are you fucking serious, Special Agent Odacio? Take a wild guess."

He thought for a minute. "Does it have to be about ourselves?"

"It's more fun that way."

"But we know a lot about each other already."

"There's a lot more to this girl than meets the eye, Special Agent Odacio," she said as the bartender returned with the Pepsi and pulled out his notepad.

"I'll have the FinBurger, no cheese," Kristen said.

"Same for me."

"Great. That should be just about ten minutes."

Kristen looked up at him and said, "Are you Fin?"

"Yes. Sure am," he said, enjoying the attention. "Kevin Finnerty, but people call me Fin."

"Did you invent the FinBurger, Fin?" she asked.

"Well, to be honest, I encountered it on a trip to Vegas once, really liked it, and kind of ripped it off. That's what all food is, though, I suppose. I'd be lying if I said I invented it."

"Well, I appreciate your honesty, Fin," she said.

"Let me know if you need anything else, hon," he said as he made his way back to the bar.

"Now, where were we? I think I was about to prove that you don't know when I'm lying."

"Oh, fuck," Odacio said under his breath.

"Ok. Not the reaction I was expecting," Kristen said, rolling her eyes.

"No. Not that. It's Bonner." He had just walked through the door.

"What is bonner?" she asked as Odacio and Bonner made eye contact, and he made his way towards the table.

"Special Agent Odacio," Bonner said as he gave a brief nod. "And who is this lovely lady?"

"This is Kristen Odacio," Odacio said, making an introductory hand motion.

"Your sister?" Bonner asked.

"No. My wife."

"Honey, you sure could have done better than this guy."

"It was an arranged marriage," Kristen said, smiling.

"Oh, I like you better than him already," Bonner responded. Before Odacio could say anything else, Kristen jumped back in.

"Would you like to join us?" she asked, giving the third seat a little kick.

"In just a moment, honey. I'm going to say hello to Fin. I'll be back in a minute." He walked towards the bar.

"Why did you do that?" Odacio asked.

"Common courtesy. Just being normal."

"We were having a good time."

"Sorry. He seemed like a nice guy," Kristen said.

"He's not. He insulted me within about three seconds. Did you not notice that?"

"He was playing," she said.

"He wasn't playing. Whatever. We're going to eat our Finburgers, and that's it. I've got to get back to it anyway."

"He's coming back," she said. Bonner returned with a bourbon in hand, pulled up a chair, and reached out his hand.

"Kristen, I'm Brett, by the way. State police. I'm working this thing with your husband."

"Pleased to meet you, Brett."

"I won't stay long. I don't want to interrupt. You were probably in the middle of something," Bonner said.

"Actually, we were just about to play two truths and a lie. Do you want to play?" Kristen asked. "It's more fun with three people."

"Why not?"

"Okay. Chris, do you want to go first?" Kristen asked.

"No. One of you go."

"Ok, Brett, we don't know you; you go first," Kristen said.

"I take it I'm supposed to tell you two truths and one lie, and you'll guess which is which?" Bonner asked.

"Yes, and it's more fun if it's about you."

Bonner downed his bourbon and thought for a minute. "Ok. This is hard, but here it goes. I was an Army Ranger. That's one. I was never married. That's two. One more…"

"Give us something a little juicier, Brett. Put your mind to it," Kristen said. He paused.

"Okay. I once had relations with a woman at the courthouse," he said.

"Do you mean with a woman who worked at the courthouse, or do you mean you had relations *in* the courthouse?" Kristen asked.

"The latter."

"Okay, this is fun. I'll guess first," Kristen said. "I think you are telling the truth about the courthouse. That rolled off your tongue. I'm going to say you were an army ranger and you have been married. And so that's the lie. I think you're divorced. Chris, what do you think?"

"I'll give him relations in the courthouse as a truth. But I don't believe for one minute that any woman ever married this guy. At the risk of offending, I'm going to say that you were not an Army Ranger," Odacio said.

"You win, Agent Odacio. Navy Seal. Two tours. Your turn."

"Okay. I gotta do it in a way where Kristen doesn't have an unfair advantage."

"Actually, I have to use the ladies room. You two keep at it," she said as she got up and walked towards the bathroom.

"Ok. That makes it easier. US Army, stationed in Germany. Fluent in three languages. Never drew my weapon in the line of duty," Odacio said as he finished his Pepsi.

Bonner signaled to Fin for a refill. "Army, but no combat experience. The service would give you a leg up getting into the FBI. True. Chasing white-collar criminals, hackers… never drew your weapon, also true. I'm guessing you are fluent in four languages, not three. Your statement about languages is false," Bonner said as Fin topped him off and headed back to the bar.

"I picked up Spanish from my father. I studied and picked up German in the service. My English is pretty good too. That statement is true," Odacio said as Kristen returned to the table.

"What did I miss?" she asked.

"Me winning," Odacio said. "Your turn. You want me to take

a walk and make it fair?"

"No. I've got this. Okay. Once I won $5000 on a $50 bet. I moved three times as a kid, but each time my room was the exact same size. I once held an intruder at gunpoint until the police arrived."

"Oh, whatever. I'll let Bonner go first," Odacio said.

"Alright. That's pretty good, Kristen. But I think I got a read on you. You grew up living in a trailer home, moved around a lot in that trailer. True. Your daddy took you with him to the track pretty often. He couldn't afford a babysitter. You placed enough bets over the years to win a longshot, but you didn't have $50 to bet on horses. You had $5 or fifty cents something like that. Maybe you won $500. The statement is false. You seem like a tough, smart cookie. You have access to your husband's firearms. You held an intruder at gunpoint. True," Bonner said as he took a sip of his bourbon.

"Forget about it," Odacio began. "You never held an intruder at gunpoint. We would have talked about that. Hats off, Bonner, on deducing the trailer and horse track. When did you win $5000?" he asked Kristen.

"Final answer?" she asked.

"Yes," Odacio said.

"Brett wins," Kristen said and smiled wryly. Bonner raised his glass, tipped it, and took another swig.

"What are you talking about, Kristen?" Odacio balked.

"It's obvious the way she carries herself, Odacio, she can take care of herself. Maybe you two oughta trade gigs."

"Fuck off, Bonner," he said, turning attention back to Kristen. "What are you talking about? You would have told me about that by now."

"I'm sorry. It happened once. It's not a big deal. I had to

reach to come up with things that you don't know about me."

"It is a big deal. When did that happen?"

"A long time ago," she said, as Fin approached the table with the Fin Burgers, interrupting the tension.

Bonner finished his bourbon. "I'm going to need another one, but I'll come to the bar Fin, let these two enjoy dinner together. I wanted to talk to you anyways. Odacio, it was a tie. I got you wrong, but I got her right. We'll rematch someday. Are we getting back to it after you eat?"

"Fine. Yeah," Odacio said, still a little annoyed. Bonner gave a little salute to Kristen and followed Fin back to the bar.

"What was that?" Odacio asked.

"Sorry. I didn't realize it would strike a nerve."

"It did, and you should have realized."

"That's fair."

"You don't know that guy. I don't know that guy. I don't like hearing things I haven't heard before about you, in front of a fucking stranger, especially something meaningful like that."

"I get it. I'm sorry. We were playing two truths and a lie. I wanted to win," Kristen said. They sat in silence eating their Fin Burgers for a few minutes, Odacio eating fast.

"Again. I'm sorry. I didn't mean to ruin our dinner," she said.

"You didn't ruin it. The FinBurger is good."

"I should have told you when it happened."

He put down his burger, paused, and looked up. "This happened when we were together? And you didn't tell me?" he asked, annoyed again but calmer than before.

"It happened when you were on leave helping your mother. I didn't tell you because I didn't want to worry you and have you come home. She needed you then; your stepfather had just passed," she said.

"Details," he said.

"It really was nothing. Your car was gone. I was out, and the mailbox was overflowing. The house looked like we were on vacation. Some junkie, he didn't even have a weapon. It was a crime of opportunity sort of thing. I heard him upstairs when I came in the back door. I dialed 911 immediately. I should have left quietly right then, but I pulled the gun and sat at the kitchen table. He came down, and I surprised him and told him to take a seat. We sat there about five awkward minutes, and the cops showed up. That was the end of that. I've been locking the door since."

"Jesus, Kristen. In case this isn't crystal clear, or if there is any lack of certainty about it, if something like that happens, I expect you to fucking call me. I don't care what the fuck is going on otherwise. I can't believe I even have to be saying this."

"I promise. Scout's honor."

"You weren't a fucking girl scout!"

"I know. Stop pretending to stay mad at me. You can't," she said, taunting him.

"I'm not."

"I know you're not."

"I mean I'm not pretending!" Odacio said.

"Yes, you are. Come on." She was right. He cracked a smile and let out a muffled laugh.

"Fine. Just don't do it again," he said.

"I'm heading home. You'll pay for dinner?"

"Sure. See you tonight." She grabbed her bag and walked out of Fins. Bonner watched her leave, signaled to Fin for a refill, and made his way back to Odacio's table.

"Quite a woman, Odacio. You must be doing something

right," Bonner said.

"Why do you have to insult me even when you're compliment-ing me? What the fuck did I do to you?" Odacio responded.

"Don't take it personal."

"What does that even mean? Of course I'm going to take it personally! Fuck. Just forget it. I'll tell you what, the plot really fucking thickened since I last saw you. I've got a lot to download. What about the woman?" Odacio asked.

"Inconsequential. It was fucking meaningless," Bonner said.

"What do you mean?" Odacio asked.

"I mean, the guy died for no reason. He was a just working stiff who was there by chance. She wanted him to pick up dinner. She was pretty broken up. It was a tough scene."

"She was the wife of one of our caucasian John Does?" Odacio asked.

"No. Haitian. Roseline Pierre. The husband, Stevenson, was our black John Doe," Bonner said.

"First name?" Odacio asked.

"I just told you his fucking name. Stevenson. Stevenson Pierre," Bonner said.

"Okay, calm down. Now my trip to the District Attorney's office, are you ready for this?" Odacio asked.

"Frankly, no," Bonner said.

"What do you mean? That was a rhetorical question."

"I'm not in the mood. It's late. I don't need my mind racing," Bonner said.

"Ok. Whatever," Odacio scoffed.

"I was on the end of an overtime shift, just about to end when that bomb went off. I'm several bourbons in. There ain't nothing you gonna tell me tonight that's gonna change anything or bring her back to life," Bonner said.

"Who's her?" Odacio asked.

"Who you think I'm talking about, that ADA," Bonner said.

"I didn't say anything about a woman," Odacio said.

"Whatever, I heard it earlier," Bonner said. "Let's get out of here and go home." Odacio left more than enough cash on the table, and they got up and walked out.

"Where did you park?" Odacio asked.

"Three blocks down on Main," Bonner said.

"Same." They walked towards their cars together but not talking. As they approached, Bonner's car looked lopsided.

"Fuck. Flat tire," Bonner said.

"I'll help," Odacio said.

"Don't need none," Bonner said.

"All the same, I'll wait and make sure you get off okay," Odacio responded.

"You wanna help? Fine." He pulled out his key and clicked the trunk button to pop it. "Get that doughnut out the back. I'll get the jack under the driver's seat."

Odacio walked around the back of the car. He pulled out a small flashlight, and put it in his mouth, shining it on the tire, which needed to be unscrewed to be released. As he was working it, Bonner had gotten the jack and had come around back. Odacio, not realizing it, was startled when he saw Bonner over his shoulder.

"Fuck," he said as the flashlight dropped into the trunk. "Don't sneak up on me like that. It's creepy." As Odacio grabbed the flashlight, he noticed the light pointed at something in the back corner of the trunk. It was a handgun and a bag of white powder. "What the fuck is that?!"

"What the fuck is what?" Bonner asked.

"What the fuck is that?" Odacio repeated, pointing the

flashlight at the gun and bag.

"That's nothing. Just get the fucking doughnut or get out of my way," Bonner said.

"I know exactly what that is. It's a fucking insurance policy. Isn't it!?" Odacio yelled.

"Don't you fucking judge me, boy. You sit behind your desk at your fucking computer all day. I'll fucking whoop you good," Bonner said.

"You know. Maybe ten or twenty years ago, you might have 'whooped me good,' but you've gotten old, Brett. You're slower. Your bones have less calcium, more brittle. You're an old man now, not to mention drunk. You wanna go, we can go! I'll even give you the first…" Before he could get the word out, Bonner clocked him with a right cross, sending Odacio tumbling back as he tripped on the curb. He fell awkwardly into two garbage cans, knocking them over like bowling pins, spreading garbage on the sidewalk and Odacio. He jerked his jaw around a little trying to get it realigned, and got back on his feet. Bonner came at him again. Same punch, a right-cross, but this time Odacio stepped out of the way, and Bonner's momentum, combined with his blood-alcohol level, sent him falling face-first into his tail light, shattering it.

"Your rear tail light is out, Bonner. I'm letting you off with a warning this time. See you in the morning, *asshole*. I'll be here tomorrow morning at eight." Odacio walked to his car as Bonner slowly got on his feet and lit a cigarette.

6

Chapter 6

Odacio worked through most of the night, reading the American Dawn case file at his kitchen table, eventually falling asleep there around sunrise. He awoke an hour or so later to the sound of the coffee maker and Kristen grabbing mugs. She was wearing an oversized t-shirt, one of his.

"Good morning, Agent Odacio," she said, smiling. She poured the coffee and brought it over to him. "Did you and Brett have a good time after I left?"

"Yeah."

The toaster popped. She began buttering. "Why are you giving me that look?" she asked as she put a piece of toast in front of him.

He didn't think he was giving her any look. "Huh?"

"Like you're skeptical or something?"

"You're seeing things. I don't know what you're talking about."

"I've been with you long enough to know when you're giving me a look, and you're giving me a look," she said. He took a bite of toast and grimaced. "What's wrong? Too much butter?"

"It's fine. It's good," he said.

"You're looking at me side-eyed and grunting."

He realized what was going on. "Sorry. I think I slept weird. There's something wrong with my jaw. It feels out of whack."

"Let me look at it," she said.

"No. It's fine. Leave it…"

"I'm a nurse." She walked over and tilted his head back and felt his jaw, manipulated it a little, and before he could indicate that it hurt, gave it a quick hard jerk, causing a loud click sound that they both heard.

"Fuck!" he said, his hand twitching with the pain knocking his coffee onto his toast. "What the fuck was that?"

"Jesus, it was like you got your jaw out of the socket or something. Don't sleep on the kitchen table again."

"Don't worry. I won't."

"We're good, yeah?" she asked.

"Huh?"

"The junkie, intruder thing."

"We're fine." Odacio got up and fed Frank, who came into the kitchen when he heard all the commotion. He scarfed it down.

"Are you going to walk him this morning, or do you need me to?" Kristen asked. Frank, hearing the word walk started to get excited.

"What time is it?"

"7:45."

"I'm late, do you mind?"

"No. Call me later," she said. Odacio got up, went to the bathroom, brushed his teeth, splashed water on his face, and changed clothes. He headed out to the Cherokee.

When he arrived downtown, Bonner was there already, standing outside his car smoking a cigarette just as he'd left him the previous night.

"You're late," Bonner said.

"It's 8:07," Odacio said.

"Yeah, it is," Bonner said. "Have you eaten breakfast?"

"Yeah. Kind of."

"Well, I haven't. Follow me." They walked a block down to a small deli with a few tables. Bonner ordered a bacon, egg, and cheese sandwich and a coffee. Odacio got another cup of coffee. They sat down in the corner, both going for the seat facing the door; Bonner took it. "I have information. But give me what you got first; I'm ready for it now."

"Alright. I met with the folks at the DA's office. Ron Peters and two of his ADAs."

"Which ones?"

"Kate Peters and Bobby Sokolov."

"Sokolov? He's a fucking Communist."

"Jesus, Brett. Because his parents or grandparents were Russian? You know a lot of Russians fled communism to come to this country, risking their lives."

"Not because he's Russian," Bonner growled, raising his voice, "because he's a goddamn fucking communist!" Two customers in line gave them a look.

"You know him?" Odacio asked.

"I know all of them."

"Brooke Littman?"

Bonner paused. "I knew her. She's the female Jane Doe?"

"Yeah. It wasn't an accident that she was there. She got a call yesterday morning, someone claiming to be an American Dawn defector, with recordings of their meetings. He said they were planning something terrible and that hundreds of people were going to die. They arranged to meet at Nellie's for a handoff."

"Her idea or his?" Bonner asked.

"They don't know for sure. Brooke recounted the conversation to Kate and Bobby, but they don't remember that detail or whether she said one way or another."

"What do you make of it?" Bonner asked.

"The most plausible thing, I think, is that the defector was bogus, a pretext to get her to a specific place at a specific time. It could have been one of the ringleaders or a lieutenant at American Dawn posing as a defector. I think they're behind this," Odacio said.

"I know those boys. The papers blew everything out of proportion."

"What are you saying?" Odacio asked.

"I'm saying it don't smell right. It doesn't add up for me."

"Brooke handled the Brody Wilcox case; they were going to plea out this week. Maybe they were trying to buy time, something to derail that?"

"By incriminating themselves in a bombing? That would be quite the escalation. A lot of people see their side of things; this would change public opinion right quick."

"What do you mean people see their side of things? You mean with Brody's case?" Odacio asked.

"Yeah. You familiar with the case?"

"Read the file last night," Odacio said.

"You ever been out on Lake Drive?"

"No," Odacio said.

"There are about four houses on it, long country road, no through traffic. Brody driving home, about a hundred feet from his driveway, sees two parked cars on the side of the road. Strangers. Maybe he wanted to see if they were lost; maybe he thought they were a threat. Bottom line, they didn't belong there."

"He could have called the police," Odacio said.

"It's on the outskirts. Could be it would take a cop thirty minutes to show up. This ain't the city. People here need firearms, and they need to be able to protect themselves. Think about how things might have gone different with Kristen and that intruder. Very easily could be that Kristen is sitting in that cell."

"Totally different situation. That was an intruder, a burglar in our house. This was two guys parked on the side of the road minding their own business," Odacio said.

"I know it's different, but it's not wildly different. That road is practically his property. There's only four families who live there. Brody's a hothead; he should do time. I'm not saying otherwise. But the bottom line is if those boys hadn't been where they weren't supposed to be, doing something they weren't supposed to do, the one would still be alive, and the other wouldn't have metal in his belly."

"So what do you make of American Dawn?" Odacio asked.

"Shit. It's a fucking hunting club with a Facebook page."

"And a million dollars in its bank account."

"That's the media's doing. Doesn't change the fundamentals."

"Which are?" Odacio asked.

"As I said, Brody's a hothead, also dimwitted. Keith Brown, he's smart, but he's a fucking coward. A lot more bark than bite. That million dollars ain't gonna last, and it's probably half gone already. Keith's been spending it on trips to conferences and Trump rallies. He goes in style, not to mention all them ads he takes out in the *Freeman*."

"Well, what do you make of the defector then, the claim that they were planning to kill hundreds of people?" Odacio asked.

"I don't know yet, but you ask me now, I say maybe a smokescreen," Bonner said.

"A smokescreen masterminded by Jermaine?" Odacio asked.

"I don't know, but there's more to it. While you two were eating your burgers last night, I got talking to Fin."

"Yeah, and?" Odacio asked.

"Well, it sounds like our two caucasian John Does might be the Conejo brothers," Bonner said.

"Is that supposed to mean something to me?"

"The Conejo brothers. Matthew and Jerry Ramos. I collared Jerry more than once, one of them stuck. Did five years. Never got Matthew, but he's a known quantity too."

"What are they into?" Odacio asked.

"Opioids mostly, but anything to make a buck. I got Jerry for armed robbery of a local grocery store. The fucking idiot, no less than three people in the store at the time knew him personally and were able to ID him."

"What did Fin say about it?"

"There wasn't much to it. Jerry was waiting around for Matthew. Matthew shows up, doesn't order anything, says they got business at Nellie's. The two leave together."

"Why didn't Fin report that to your officers? I assume he was canvassed."

"That's a long story, but it ain't relevant right now. Fact is, we had quite the cast of characters in Nellie's at 4 p.m. yesterday. Oh, and one more thing, when Jerry did time, that was Brooke's case too."

"Fuck, that's strange. And the Conejo brothers, are they

Latino?" Odacio asked.

"Hell, no. They're white. Local boys."

"You think they might have business or something going on with American Dawn?"

"It's possible. But they run in different circles. I'd be surprised if they knew each other," Bonner said.

"We need phone records for Keith Brown and the Conejos," Odacio said.

"It would be Matthew doing the talking. But I don't think Keith has anything to do with this."

"I can ask Jackie to see what he can do," Odacio said.

"Who's Jackie?"

"ASAC Jackie Davis," Odacio said.

"You report to a woman?"

"No."

"Jackie's a woman's name," Bonner said.

"It's unisex."

"I never heard of a man named Jackie," Bonner said.

"What about Jackie Robinson? I think he was named after Jackie Robinson," Odacio said.

"Oh."

"Oh, what?"

"ASAC Davis is a black man,"

"Yeah, so what?"

"So nothing. ASAC Davis is a black man, that's all."

"What are you pointing it out for?"

"We're just talking; you brought it up."

"I didn't bring up anything," Odacio said.

"Fine. Leave it alone, then. I'm going to sniff around the Conejo angle. See what they been up to and who might want to get them these days."

"I'm going to pay a visit to the Browns and Brody, see what I can find out."

"Sounds good. Meet back at Fin's tonight, 6 p.m. to compare notes," Bonner said

"Alright, six. Oh, Bonner…" Odacio said as he was getting up from the table. "Jackie Gleason."

"What about him?"

"He was a white guy."

7

Chapter 7

Odacio walked back alone to his Cherokee. He pulled out the Wilcox case file and thumbed through it until he found Keith Brown's address, as he remembered he was interviewed in conjunction with that case. Using voice command, he put Keith's address into his GPS and started driving. Then he called Jackie.

"This is ASAC Davis."

"It's Scout, sir."

"Good morning. What's new?"

"We've got a lead on our two caucasian John Does. They're brothers, well-known local criminals known as the Conejo brothers, heavily into opioids. One of them did a stint on armed robbery."

"That adds a layer of complexity. They could easily be the marks," Jackie said.

"Possibly. I need to find a connection between the Conejos and American Dawn."

"There may or may not be a connection there, Scout."

"I'm hoping to get our hands on Matthew Ramos' phone

records. He's one of the criminals."

"I'll see what I can do."

"Keith Brown is the leader of American Dawn. We need his phone records as well, and anything else we can get on him, like a warrant to search the premises," Odacio said.

"You're getting ahead of yourself. There's nothing that ties Keith Brown to this yet. All we have is an anonymous caller claiming to be from American Dawn. No judge would give us that warrant."

"Alright. Do you have anything for me on Brooke or Jermaine?"

"By the end of the day, I think. I'll let you know as soon as we do," Jackie said.

"There's another detail. One of the brothers, the one who did time on armed robbery... that was Brooke's case."

"So Brooke Littman, the ADA, is sitting in a restaurant with two criminals, one of whom she sent up the river. There's one other person there. What's his connection?" Jackie asked.

"None. We think he was a random walk-in."

"Okay, on the connection between the criminal and the ADA, any theories on that?"

"Not yet. I'm focused on the connection between the Conejo brothers and American Dawn at the moment," Odacio said.

"You should look for any connection, not just connections with American Dawn," Jackie said.

"Roger that, sir."

"Call me when you have an update."

"Yessir." Odacio continued driving, passing a general store and a few farms, keeping his eye out for Long Branch Road, where Keith Brown lived. The GPS voice told him he'd arrive at his destination in eight minutes. About six minutes later, his phone rang; it was a local number but not one he recognized.

"This is Special Agent Odacio."

"This is Sonia Gonzales from the *Daily Freeman*. I'm writing a story on Nellie's and the connection to American Dawn."

"What connection to American Dawn?" Odacio asked.

"That's why I am calling; I'd like to ask you a few questions," she said.

"If you have information on the explosion, please share it. What have you heard?" Odacio asked.

"I'm calling to ask *you* questions. Are you investigating American Dawn in conjunction with the explosion at Nellie's?"

"What have you heard?" he repeated.

"I've heard that American Dawn is involved. Are you or aren't you leading an investigation into American Dawn?" She repeated.

"I'm not going to comment."

"My deadline is 3 p.m. in case you change your mind. I called you from my cell phone; you can reach me at this number any time."

Odacio pressed the 'end call' button. He thought to himself that must have come from the DA's office. Kate? Bobby? He decided to worry about it later as he turned onto Long Branch Road.

"Your destination is on the left," the GPS voice said. Odacio pulled into the long driveway, the house not visible from the road. A sign on one of the trees read, "WARNING: ADMINIS-TRATION OF PRIVATE JUSTICE ON THIS PROPERTY." Another one read "LIVE FREE OR DIE." The house was a double-wide trailer with a half-finished covered porch that was under construction. Next to the house was a brand new prefab barn that looked more valuable than the house.

As he pulled his car to a stop, a man, presumably Brown, emerged from the doorway rifle in hand but pointed towards the ground. Odacio rolled down his window but didn't open the car door. "Mr. Brown, I'm Special Agent Odacio, FBI; I'd like to have a word with you."

Keith Brown nodded and put the rifle down, leaning against the trailer, and approached the vehicle as Odacio stepped out. "You're Keith Brown, I assume?" Odacio asked while putting his hand out to shake, Brown, obliging. Keith Brown was about fifty years old with a grey beard and mustache. He looked kind of like a meaner Kenny Rogers, with a nasty scratch from his right eye down to the beard.

"Yes. You said your name was…?"

"Special Agent Odacio."

"I hope you won't be offended if I don't invite you inside."

"Not a problem. We can talk right here," Odacio said.

"Let's walk and talk. I'll show you around the property," Brown said, motioning for him to follow as they walked towards the backyard and onto a wooded path.

"I noticed your barn on the way in. I was thinking of buying one of those but haven't gotten around to it."

"I thought about doing it myself, but the Amish do a great job. Fine workmanship. I assume you're not here to admire my barn, though. We can walk along the creek, and you can tell me to what I owe this unexpected visit."

"I need to ask you a few questions about American Dawn."

"Have we caught the attention of the FBI already? We saying things you all don't want to be said?"

"We don't care about what you say. It's what you do or might do."

"You and I know that's not the case, Agent Odacio. The first

53

amendment, it's not for everyone anymore, wouldn't you say?"

"No, I wouldn't. "

"Well, it's for everyone until they start saying the wrong things. Things that the newspapers, the facebooks, and the deep state don't like. Well, that's beyond the bounds of the first amendment these days, it seems to me."

"You're free to set up your websites and your pages; you say what you want."

"Yeah, and then I get a visit from an armed agent of the federal government. Have you visited any Democrat Socialists recently?"

"I don't work every case."

"Who in your office is assigned to Antifa? Is it one agent? Is it two agents? Or is it none?"

"There's not any Antifa activity in this region. We follow the facts and threats. If Antifa were planning something illegal, we'd be on them like white on rice."

"So is that it? You're on me because you think I'm going to do something, not because I have done something? I'll be guilty eventually of something, so might as well get me now?"

"I'm not here to get you, Mr. Brown. I'm here to get your side of the story. Tell me about American Dawn. What're you fighting for?"

"You see, even there, you say you want my side of the story, like as if I've done something that I haven't done. You want to know about American Dawn, I'll tell you, but I'd appreciate a presumption of innocence for whatever it is you are up my ass about."

"Poor choice of words. Tell me about American Dawn, sir," Odacio said as they stepped up to the top of the hill and into a clearing.

"Would you look at that view," Brown said, looking out at a majestic mountain range in the distance. "Beautiful, isn't it?"

"It is. It's amazing."

"This was my daddy's land, and his daddy's before that, and his before that. Someday it will be Juniors. But this land is *my* land. It's not *your* land. It's not *our* land. It's *my* land. Kole County taxes it like it's their land. We've got seven acres here. The county tells me I can't build a barn on my land without their permission. The state government tells me certain animals I can't kill on my land even though they're trespassing. The federal government tells me which guns I can and cannot shoot those animals with or protect my family with. Maybe I have a falling out with Junior, and I want to sell my land. Well, now I got the government telling me I gotta be willing to sell it to illegal immigrants or some black family with a criminal record like I'm supposed to be color blind. Does that sound like freedom to you, Agent Odacio?"

"It's a free country, Mr. Brown. But it's also a society and a democracy. And democracies make rules and laws."

"Democracy? Wake up, Agent Odacio! Our freedoms, our way of life is being stolen away from us. It's death by a thousand cuts. Even Trump can't stop it. Everything that man tries to do, they get in the way. If it's not Congress, it's courts, if it's not courts, it's deep state bureaucrats, if it ain't them, it's Hollywood brainwashing the public or Twitter deciding what is and isn't appropriate to be said or heard. There's a war brewing, has been for years."

"Has it?"

"Ruby Ridge, Waco, them folks out in Portland. Nothing less than the freedom and ideals this country was founded on are at stake. And people are starting to wake up. A new American

Dawn is needed in this country. You ask me what we're about? That's what we're about — the ideal of the USA!"

"And stockpiling weaponry?" Odacio asked.

"You're damn right we are. This country is a powder keg. We're on the verge of a second civil war. Fracture. A new start. A fresh start. But blood will spill first, and we're going to be ready for it. People are going to have to choose sides, Agent Odacio. You'll see. Where you gonna be? With the communists, Antifa, the blacks, the illegals? Or are you going to fight for your country?"

"I signed up to fight for my country, first in the Army, now with the FBI."

"FBI? Forget it - you all are part of the problem. You pick and choose who you go after, and you come for real Americans like me and my family!"

"Speaking of family, what's Junior's role in American Dawn?" Odacio asked.

"Junior gonna run it one day. He's just started training now." Brown said.

"Training?" Odacio asked.

"Shipped off to the US Marine Corps on Monday, the finest fighting force on earth. He's at the recruit depot on Parris Island."

"You have him join the Marine Corp to train to run American Dawn?" Odacio asked.

"Junior makes his own decisions. Been wanting to be a Marine since he was ten years old. American Dawn is a peaceful organization, Odacio, but we're also preparing for what we know is coming. We'll be on the frontlines when it happens, and we need trained military men to run our operations when the time comes. We're operating within the bounds of the law, and well within our rights, that is, if we still have any rights."

"How do I go about signing up to join American Dawn?" Odacio asked.

"Fuck you, Odacio. You'd never make the cut. It's by invitation only. We recruit *real* Americans," Brown said.

"What makes a real American, Mr. Brown?" Odacio asked.

"You know, maybe you'd be better off trying to figure out who blew up that restaurant downtown than you are sniffing around me and my business."

"Could be I already am."

"Well fuck you then. Get off my land. You come back here; you bring a warrant or about twenty of your boys packing, and let's see what happens. I've extended all the courtesy to the federal government that I intend to," Brown said.

"I can walk myself out. It's been a pleasure, Mr. Brown," Odacio said. Brown turned his back and stared out at the mountain range as Odacio made his way back to the Cherokee. The walk back was about a hundred yards. As he came up the path towards the driveway, another car was pulling in and parked, and a tall, large woman got out of the car.

"Can I help you?" she said.

"No, ma'am. I was just leaving. Your husband was showing me around the property. He's still up at the clearing with that spectacular view of the mountains. I'm Special Agent Odacio, FBI. Nice to make your acquaintance." They approached each other, and as they did, he noticed a thick layer of makeup covering up what looked to be a faded bruise on her cheek.

"You have a warrant?" she asked.

"No, ma'am."

"Well, go on then. Go on."

"Yes, ma'am. I'm going to leave my card in case your husband wants it or if you ever need anything," Odacio said. She just kept walking towards the door. "It's on your windshield."

8

Chapter 8

Odacio got in the Cherokee, did a k-turn, and then drove up the long driveway back towards the road. When he got off the property and onto Long Branch, he pulled over and reset his GPS to go to the county jail. It was on the border of Kole and neighboring Birch County as they shared one "county" jail between them to save money. From where he was coming, it was all backroads and easily an hour's drive. He pulled up an 80's station on Pandora and got a song or two in before losing service and turned to the radio, finding a country station that came through well enough.

When he arrived, he was chastised by the guards for not calling ahead. They said it would be a while. But the internet worked there, so he used the time to search on his phone and read all the American Dawn articles he could find. One article mentioned that American Dawn met on the third Saturday of the month. If there was actually a defector, he thought to himself; he might be able to figure out who it was if he could listen in on the meeting this coming Saturday. Jackie didn't think the defector was real, but they hadn't discounted that possibility completely yet. Getting a warrant for a wire would be tough, if not impossible. He looked at his watch and realized it was after 3 p.m., and he'd been waiting two hours. Just then, a guard called him and brought him to a private room with a table and two chairs. "He'll be out momentarily," the guard said.

As Brody approached, he was unrecognizable from the photos. In the newspaper and mugshots, he had long dark curly hair and a full beard and mustache. He looked a little like Mick Foley, the professional wrestler from some years back who went by the ring name Mankind. The man approaching had a goatee, but his head was shaved, and his arms were covered in tattoos.

"Brody Wilcox?" Odacio asked as he sat down.

"Yeah. Who's asking?"

"Special Agent Odacio, FBI."

"What on earth does the FBI want with me?"

"Just to ask you a few questions."

"I don't have my lawyer present."

"I can make an appointment and come back."

"What's this about? The case is over as far as I know."

"What's the status of your plea deal?" Odacio asked.

"As far as I know, we're waiting on that bitch ADA. Sweating us or something," Brody said.

"You might be waiting a while," Odacio said.

"Oh yeah, why's that?"

"The day before yesterday, there was an explosion downtown. Brooke Littman was one of the victims."

"She's dead? Well fuck. Not sure what to make of that. I guess I might be waiting longer to hear back?"

"I don't know. I assume someone in the office picks up where she left off," Odacio said.

"Well, they better pick it up quick. You come all the way down here to tell me that bitch is dead?"

"Being an ADA, there's a long list of people who might have a score to settle with her," Odacio said.

"Shit, man, you trying to pin this shit on me? I'm in a goddamn cage most all day, got these guards watching my every goddamn move. Video cameras everywhere. You think I slipped outta here, killed her, and came back?" Brody asked sarcastically.

"No. But you garnered a lot of support in the community. Maybe someone acting on your behalf or behalf of the cause?"

"Fuck the cause. That ain't got nothing to do with me. I agree with some of that stuff, but I ain't political. Leave me alone, let me go hunting, let me make my way in life. I don't even read the newspaper. That's more Keith's thing. We had our club; some of the guys like to get deep into the politics. Others don't. I'm one of the others. They're just using me to make their point," Brody said.

"What's their point, Brody?"

"Their point is that people should keep with their own. I don't roll up into black neighborhoods casing the joint, and they shouldn't roll up into mine. Some of them have their QANON. Some of them have their Jew thing. Hillary this. Obama that. It's a bunch of hunting snipe."

"What's snipe?"

"You know. Like what do they say? A fool's errand, one dude playing tricks on another. There ain't no such thing as snipe, so you ain't gonna be able to kill one. Like all this shit about child sex trafficking and Hillary Clinton. Fuck that bitch, but she ain't trafficking no children; it's a goddamn fantasy. Like too many people my age not knowing how to navigate the goddamn internet or something."

"Brody, a bomb went off downtown and killed at least four people. Do you think American Dawn would be capable of something like that?"

"Capable? Sure. They got guys with the know-how, the expertise. A lot of former military men gravitated to it, especially after I got locked up. But capable doesn't mean they would do it."

"It was at Nellie's Soul Kitchen, I'm thinking this has something to do with your case, Brooke Littman, and it being a black-owned business," Odacio said.

"Could be. I've heard people say things from time to time—mostly just dudes blowing smoke when they had one too many. Like one time, I won't say who, so don't ask me. One of the guys was talking about blowing up the taco shack down on Wiltshire. Man, I said, I like tacos. I don't like having all these Mexicans around, but they mostly keep to themselves, and I like tacos. It didn't go anywhere. That talk is par for the course, but that's all it is, talk. Some of these boys never even downed a buck, let alone a person."

"Who inside American Dawn is capable of something like this?" Odacio asked.

"Shit, man. What you think? We're friends? Like I'm going to confide in you. Name names? Hell, even if I wanted to say something, they'd cut my nuts off in here," Brody said.

"What if I could get you out of here, Brody. Get you moved to a minimum-security place, a Club Fed?" Odacio asked.

"Well, now we're talking. I played it straight here, but if what I know is valuable enough for you to get me into Club Fed, well, then we got something to talk about. But I would need my lawyer for a conversation like that."

"I'd need to have some conversations," Odacio said.

"Well, by all means. I've got time. Get it?"

"Yeah, I get it. It might be a few days, and it might not work out, but we'll see." Odacio got up from the table and nodded his head, signaling the guard. On his way out, he stopped to talk to one of the guards behind the glass. "Can I see the visitor log for Brody Wilcox?"

"Wilcox has been here for over six months. We'd need to get that together. We're short-handed today. It could take a while. Do you want to wait?

"Can I leave my card, and you email it to me?" Odacio asked.

"Sure," the guard said.

Odacio made his way through the security checkpoints and back towards his car. As he walked through the lot, he checked his cell phone and saw he had five missed calls from the same number, one he didn't recognize. He dialed it back. A man answered.

"This is Special Agent Odacio; I missed a call from this number."

"You want a war? Well, now you got one, you son of bitch!"

"Who is this?" Odacio asked.

"You know damn well who this is!"

"Sorry, no."

"Keith Brown!"

"What can I do for you, Mr. Brown?"

"You ran that article in the *Daily Freeman*. It posted online, gonna be in tomorrow's paper!"

"Ah. Okay. I don't run articles in the newspaper. I don't control the media. I haven't read the article, and I didn't comment on it," Odacio said

"But you knew about it, and where did they get it? Trusted source my ass. You try to pin this on me, and you watch what happens. If there is one thing I know, it's public relations, and I'm going to have a field day with this one," Brown said.

"What does it say? I haven't read it yet."

"Some nonsense about a defector in our midst. Speculation that I put a hit out on Littman. You'll pay for this!" Brown said.

"Mr. Brown, if you had a defector, the last thing I'd want is for you to know about it. I think I'm about as annoyed by this article as you are," Odacio said.

"That's what you'd say regardless. Fuck you and fuck that Jew bitch. I'm glad she's dead. She deserved it. You made your move; now I'll make mine," Brown said before hanging up the phone. Odacio got in the Cherokee and started on the long road back. He put back on the 80's station and listened to 'dancing with myself' by Billy Idol on his way out the lot. A few miles from the jail, he had to switch back to the radio. A few songs in, his phone rang; it was Kristen.

"Hey," he said.

"Holy shit. I just read the article on my phone," she said.

"Yeah, I just heard about it."

"I called it. Those racist American Dawn people are behind the bombing."

"It's an open investigation."

"Yeah. But I totally called it," Kristen said.

"I shouldn't really talk about it."

"Yeah. I just want to say I hope you nail these bastards. I hope you drive the nail through their balls."

"I'm working on it, honey."

"Where are you?"

"Driving back from the county jail, heading to meet up with

Bonner. I think I can be home in time for a late dinner if you're willing to wait."

"Deal. I'll figure something out. Just text me with an hour's notice or so."

9

Chapter 9

Fin's was less crowded tonight. About five people at the bar, three tables filled. Odacio walked up to the bar and ordered a Pepsi and a glass of water with ice. One of the guys at the bar made a comment like 'stiff drink' or something under his breath. Odacio ignored it and grabbed an empty table. Bonner walked in, acknowledging Odacio but heading right to the bar. Fin poured Bonner a bourbon, and he threw it back. Bonner struck up a conversation with one of the guys at the bar for maybe two minutes, then signaled Fin for another bourbon before walking over to join Odacio.

"What are you drinking, kid?" Bonner asked.

"Pepsi and a glass of water," Odacio said. Bonner sighed.

"You know the boy scout routine gets old quick."

"Huh?"

"You know what I'm talking about. The boy scout routine. Your shit stinks just like everyone else's."

"Why are you always in such a bad mood?" Odacio asked. "How about starting with: hello, how was your day?"

"Listen, Scout, get used to it. You're going to have to put up with me until we see this through."

"Wait, first of all, don't call me Scout. Call me Odacio."

"Whatever you say, Scout. What's new?"

"A story in the *Freeman*."

"Yeah. I saw that. He'll deny it, but that fucking communist leaked it," Bonner said.

"I'm annoyed it leaked, but maybe it'll shake some trees."

"Keith Brown didn't order no hit on Brooke. It's a ridiculous article."

"You told me Keith Brown was a coward; what did that mean?"

"You know, not the kind of guy you want to spend time in a foxhole with," Bonner said.

"Yeah, but what do you know about him?"

"I know I've seen Lenora Brown enough times around town with bruises to know they aren't exactly happily married," Bonner said.

"I got the same impression."

"Keep in mind she's no peach either. She probably whoops on him good too, from time to time. But no matter, any man who beats on his wife is a coward in my book," Bonner said.

"Speaking of the Browns, apparently Keith Junior just shipped off to the Marine Corps yesterday. Him being out of the picture suddenly, I would find that suspicious, but you don't just up and join the Marines; that would have been a long time coming. However, it did make me think if that defector was bullshit and just a lure, who do you trust more than your son to make that call? And all the better if you know he's gone off to join the Marines. Outta sight outta mind for us sort of thing?" Odacio said.

"I'm telling you Keith Brown is not a terrorist, and he cares a lot about PR. Nobody is going to get on board with a bombing."

"He kept talking about a second civil war coming and that they were preparing. Maybe this is part of some chain of events they're trying to set off," Odacio said.

"If it's a civil war they're after, they'd need to do a lot more than blow up one soul food restaurant."

"Well, maybe that's what the defector was referring to," Odacio said.

"A civil war in which hundreds of people would die?"

"No. A series of bombings intended to start a civil war. When I was at the jail earlier, Brody said there'd been talk about blowing up the taco shop," Odacio said.

"The one down on Wiltshire? I love those tacos."

"Yeah, Brody likes them too. He was willing to talk."

"To save the taco place?"

"No!" Odacio rolled his eyes. "In return for a ticket to Club Fed."

"Now you listen good; you give that boy a ticket to Club Fed, he will tell you American Dawn was responsible for the first World Trade Center bombing, Oklahoma City, whatever you want to know, he'll feed it to you. But it won't make it true."

"I wasn't born yesterday."

"Yeah, but pretty recently still," Bonner said.

"Look, we should be considering the possibility that Nellie's was the beginning. It could be the first in a string of bombings."

"You're jumping to conclusions, but I've gotta take a shit. Occupy yourself for a bit." As Bonner passed the bar, he signaled Fin for a refill. Odacio pulled up ESPN.com and started scrolling through the headline stories. A minute later, Fin came over with Bonner's drink and set it down on the table.

"You know, you really shouldn't encourage him," Fin said.

"He certainly doesn't need any encouragement from me," Odacio said.

"All the same, I'm just saying, you shouldn't encourage him. He's going through a rough time with the bomb and all."

"I'm not encouraging him. It really has nothing to do with me," Odacio said.

"Come on, kid. Guy hasn't been in here in about ten years."

"Well, he sure looks like a regular to me."

"Picking up right where he left off. They didn't teach you to put two and two together at the Ivy League school you went to?"

"I went to a state school," Odacio said.

"What about there? They teach two plus two?"

"Okay, I catch your drift, but he's not going to listen to me. He doesn't seem to like me very much." Fin looked at him and walked back to the bar. Two articles later, Bonner returned to a full glass. He picked it up, and as he brought it to his mouth, Odacio said, "You know, maybe you ought to slow…" It wasn't a sip; it was a swig, and it was gone.

"One more," Bonner said to Fin, who was back behind the bar.

"You know, Bonner, it's early. You're going a little hard, no?"

"Quit the routine, Scout."

"I asked you not to call me that," Odacio said as Fin walked out from behind the bar with the bottle in hand and made his way towards the table.

"This is it, Brett. I'm topping you off, but this is it," Fin said.

"My money's no good here? that's what you're saying?" Bonner yelled.

"Easy Bonner, I don't think…" Odacio said.

"Brett, we've known each other a long time. You're my

friend…"

"Well, start acting that way!"

"I'm the only one here who is; this guy won't give it to you straight!" Fin said, pointing at Odacio.

"What the fuck?" Odacio fired back, giving Fin a look as Bonner got up from his seat and, in one motion, threw his glass against the wall, shattering it.

"Okay, that's enough; you're outta here!" Fin said, sounding like an umpire.

"I'm out of here?" Bonner said as he cocked his right hand. Odacio got up and tried to put space between the two men but blocked a right cross with his jaw in the process. The blow sent him stumbling about five feet back until a table got in his way, and he tumbled over it face-planting into the barroom floor.

"Fuck!" Odacio yelled.

"Sorry, Scout," Bonner said, too quietly for the man running across the bar to hear as he kicked Odacio in the ribs. Odacio let out a moan.

"What did you do that for, Paul?" Fin asked.

"I was backing up, Bonner!"

"That's not backing up a man in a fight; that's kicking a man while he's down!" Fin said, exasperated.

"You fucking assholes. I'm not in a fight!" Odacio said as he collected himself and got back to his feet. "Screw this shit. I'm going home. Bonner! Same rendevous tomorrow and quit punching me in the fucking face!" Fin gave Bonner a look and nod as if to say, yeah, you probably should.

"Hey Scout, don't you want to know what I found out today?"

"No. I'm going home!" Odacio yelled as he left.

Odacio pulled into his driveway and walked in through the

garage. "Honey, is that you? You were supposed to give me a heads up. You're home early," Kristen called from the other room. He hung up his coat. She walked over to greet him. "What's going on? Your face is all crooked again."

"It's fine."

"It's not fine. Did you fall asleep again?"

"No. just leave it alone," he said.

"I'm snapping it back into place." Before he had a chance to object, she had her hand around his jaw and gave it a quick, hard jerk. A loud click sound again, and a louder moan by Odacio. "All better. Did that hurt?"

"Yes. A lot," he said

"I think you need to go to the dentist. You might need some sort of braces for your jaw, I think."

"I'm not going to the dentist, and I'm not getting braces. I'll be fine."

"You're not fine. Something's wrong, and you better tell me the truth about what's going on."

"Okay, fine. It's Bonner," he said.

"What do you mean? The man is beating you?'

"No! He's not beating me, Kristen!"

"This is twice in a row you've come home with your jaw near about broken! What's going on?"

"It's complicated."

"What?"

"It's a long story," he said.

"We're calling your union rep first thing tomorrow."

"No, we are not calling my union rep! Kristen, for the love of God, I can handle this. It's not a big deal. It was just... it was an accident."

"You realize you sound like a battered woman?"

71

"It was… I'm telling you… I don't want to talk about it," Odacio said.

"I swear, if this happens again, I'm calling your union rep. I met him at the Christmas Party last year."

"Kristen, if you call my union rep, we're getting a divorce! Bonner is not even in my union, and it was an accident."

"Fine. What do you want to eat tonight?"

"I'm in the mood for tacos, but I don't think I can chew."

10

Chapter 10

At 6:30 a.m., Odacio took Frank for a run. About a hundred yards into the wooded area behind the Odacios' house, there was an old railroad line that Kole County had converted into a public trail. Originally, the line was used to transport cement from mines down to the river in the 19th and early 20th centuries. Many of the old cement mines along the trail were still intact, though somewhat dilapidated. Chris and Frank would usually run out to the third ruin, about three miles out, and then turn back. But they didn't get that far today as Frank was losing steam. They stopped to rest, and Odacio's cell phone rang. Surprised to get a call so early, he looked at the screen and saw it was Jackie.

"Good morning, Scout."

"Good morning, sir."

"I'm sorry I didn't call yesterday; something came up that slowed us down. I've got the dossiers on Jermaine Childs and Brooke Littman, but I've got more than that."

"What do we know, sir?"

"We pinpointed the call that Littman got on Monday. Turns

out it wasn't a burner phone. The owner of the phone is a seventy-nine-year-old man named Sidney Farkus. He lives in a nursing home in California."

"An old man in a nursing home?"

"I know. It's strange. I've got a call into Bruno Calcetti, ASAC at the Sacramento office. They'll pay a visit to Farkus and see what they can learn. For now, all we can do is wait. On Littman, she's got an impressive resume and a list of criminals she's put away that reads like a scroll," Jackie said.

"Can you send me the list?"

"No need, I've got it covered. We're going to narrow it down to violent criminals who aren't behind bars. If this is a case of revenge, there's a decent shot it's someone on this list."

"Okay, so you don't need anything from me on that?"

"No. And there's a hotter lead for you to follow anyways. Jermaine Childs."

"Seriously?" Odacio asked.

"His file is waiting in your email. I don't have time to brief you at the moment, but it's all there. I need to tell you something else. "

"Okay. What?"

"We've been monitoring chatter on the internet related to American Dawn and by handles who have visited their pages. After that story broke in the *Freeman*, there was a spike. Keith Brown posted a diatribe about Feds coming on his property, and he screenshotted your business card to back up his story. He said you threatened him."

"He's a liar. He showed me around his property and did his manifesto thing."

"There's more. His keyboard warriors did some sleuthing. They posted your home address online, and someone said,

'Let's see how he likes it if we show up on his property.'"

"Dirtbags. The neighbors are going to *love* us if a bunch of nut jobs start protesting outside my house," Odacio said.

"Yeah, and that's probably all it would be, but take precautions. I should get going."

"Yessir. I also need to talk to you about Brody Wilcox, but it can wait. Let's talk later."

"Stay safe, Scout."

Chris and Frank did a light jog back to the house. Frank was wagging his tail, but Odacio was stewing. When they got back, Odacio decided to leave Frank in the fenced-in yard to cool off. He brought out Frank's breakfast, and a big bowl of water then went inside and showered. After suiting up, he went down to the kitchen, poured a cup of coffee, and sat down at the table in the breakfast nook with Kristen.

"How was your run?" she asked.

"Good. Frank didn't make it as far as we usually do. Maybe he *is* getting fat."

"Maybe leave him outside today, let him run around in the yard," Kristen suggested.

"Yeah, I was planning to."

"Do you need anything from the store?"

"What store?"

"Any store. I'm going shopping later this morning."

"What about work?" he asked.

"Remember I covered Gina's shift last week? She's covering mine today."

"Oh. You know, I was thinking of getting one of those doorbell camera things, we saw an ad for last week. Maybe you can pick that up," Odacio said.

"Chris, is this about that thing with Brett and the junkie?"

"No," he said.

"In seven years, I've never seen you even lock the door. Now you want a video camera on our front door? Maybe I should call ADT while I'm at it."

"Jesus, Kristen. You asked me if I wanted you to pick something up, and that's what popped into my head. Forget about it."

"Sorry. What are you getting all worked up about?" she said.

"My jaw hurts. My whole face hurts. I'm just in a bad mood."

"Should I schedule that visit with Dr. Kat?"

"I don't need a dentist. I just need a bag of ice and an Advil."

"Ok, I'll get that for you, and then I'm heading out."

Odacio put the compress on his face with one hand and used the other to open his laptop and pull up the Jermaine Childs file. He began to read it.

Odacio arrived early at the deli, where he and Bonner were meeting up. He ordered a coffee and oatmeal while he waited for Bonner to arrive. He tried to eat the oatmeal, but even that was hard. Bonner walked in and sat down.

"I'm sorry about last night, Scout."

"You're drinking too much."

"And you're not my mother."

"No, I'm the guy you keep punching in the face when you're drunk."

"Touche. But you don't need to give me that look."

"What look?"

"That side-eyed skeptical look."

"I'm not… it's not intentional," Odacio said. Bonner squinted and focused on Odacio's jaw.

"Lean your head back," Bonner said.

"What? No."

"Lean your head back, Scout. I've seen this a dozen times."

"Seen what?" Odacio asked as Bonner got up from his chair, moving quickly for an old man. He grabbed Odacio's hair in one hand and his jaw with the other. With one quick, hard jerk, Bonner snapped his jaw back into place. The loud clicking sound and Odacio's groan caught the attention of the other customers.

"Fuck!" Odacio said as Bonner sat down.

"See, all better."

"Bonner, if you do that again, or if you perform any other medical procedure on me, I will shoot you."

Bonner paused. "I've been shot before. It ain't so bad."

Odacio sighed. "Let's get to it. I've got updates, but I didn't get your report last night."

"We did a series of interviews with some low-lifes to find out what the Conejos were up to. They're definitely into opioids, and business is booming in Kole. Vice knows to be working their sources for more intel on them now. So what about you?" Bonner asked.

"Ok, so first thing, the phone call that Brooke got from the defector, it was from a cell phone, but it wasn't a burner. It's registered to a Sid Farkus out in California."

"I knew a Sid Farkus once in Kole. He was gayer than Paddy's pig," Bonner said.

"Paddy's pig? What does that even mean?"

"It's a saying. Paddy's pig was gay."

"Fine. Whatever. This Farkus is in California, living in a nursing home. ASAC Davis has the Sacramento office investigating."

"Nursing home? Alright, I'm thinking straight Farkus sold

or lost that phone somewhere along the way."

"Straight Farkus? What is that? We don't even know him. Let's just call him *our* Farkus," Odacio said.

"Fine. Fine. He's *our* Farkus."

"*Our Farkus*? I can't believe I'm even saying that. How do we even get into these conversations?" Odacio asked.

"Well…"

"That was rhetorical. Just leave it alone. Jackie also delivered the dossier on Littman and Childs. The Winthrop office is looking into the whereabouts and alibis of Brooke's convicts who are alive and out on parole or free men. They're starting with the murderers."

"Makes sense. That's gonna be a long list."

"Yeah. We also need to talk about Jermaine Childs."

"Who could have predicted that?" Bonner quipped.

"First, the insurance thing, I don't think it makes sense. The restaurant is insured, but the policy only provides $50,000 worth of coverage. That doesn't seem like enough money for the motive for something like this."

"Depends on your perspective. For some people who never had anything like $50,000, it can seem like a fortune," Bonner said.

"Yeah, but they could have just sold the place, no? Good location downtown, good condition, built-in customer base. Their tax filings showed it doing alright."

"Good point. Even if they couldn't quite get $50,000, they'd get close to that. This risk-reward ratio seems off."

"There's also his military record."

"That boy was military?" Bonner asked.

"Yes. Here's the thing. Take a wild guess as to what his job was in the Army?"

Bonner paused and thought for a moment. "Explosive Ordnance Disposal Specialist."

"Bingo," Odacio said.

"They teach you how they make them and how to take them apart. Son of a bitch," Bonner said.

"That's not all. Dishonorable discharge."

"What happened?"

"Don't know, but I'm sure it wasn't good," Odacio said.

"Okay. Say he makes a bomb to blow up the restaurant. He's familiar with it, knows the blast radius. He keeps himself close, but just far enough that he don't get cooked. The kid's got balls; I'll give him that. He doesn't do it for the money; like you said, he could probably have sold the place for near about as much. What's his motive?" Bonner asked.

"That's what I'm stuck on. He doesn't have any priors, so no run-ins with Brooke. Maybe this is about the Conejos, and he tries to pin it on American Dawn because he thinks of them as a white supremacist group, and they're as good a scapegoat as any?"

"Ok. Let's see what happens with the our Farkus phone. And in the meantime, we need a second visit with Jermaine," Bonner said.

"Yeah, but if he masterminded this whole thing, we've gotta be careful. If he thinks we're on to him, there's no telling what moves he'll make to cover his tracks further. We'll need a strategy," Odacio said.

"I've got a few more interviews scheduled later this morning, but maybe we reconnect and go see Jermaine this afternoon. Strategize on the way," Bonner said.

"That works. I'm planning to pay a visit to the DA's office about that leak."

"I'm telling you it was Sokolov. You ought to beat the communism out of that boy."

"I was thinking the same thing," Odacio said.

"Good morning, Odacio!" Bonner said with a laugh. "Where did the boy scout go?"

"Well, that's the last thing. After the story broke yesterday, Keith Brown started posting online, ranting about me coming on his property and threatening him. I had left my business card behind. He posted a photo of it to back up his story. Then some asshole ran with it and posted my home address. I'm expecting company," Odacio said.

"People have no decency anymore. What about Kristen? Does she know?" Bonner asked.

"I didn't tell her yet. I was going to; then we got in an argument."

"Is she at work?"

"No, she's off today."

"She shouldn't be alone in the house. I'm posting a man on your street this afternoon," Bonner said.

"Thanks. I realize I don't have your cell; give it to me so that we can reconnect later." They exchanged business cards and went their separate ways.

11

Chapter 11

Odacio got into the Cherokee and drove to the DA's office. Before getting out of the car, he looked in the mirror and said to himself, "Keep your cool, Scout." Odacio wasn't a hothead, but he knew himself well enough to know he needed to take a few deep breaths. Sokolov, assuming he was the leak, not only jeopardized the investigation but also put Kristen and Odacio in the crosshairs of an organization he considered to be a terrorist threat. He decided it was best that he meet with Ron Peters one on one first. As he walked in the front door, he was greeted by the receptionist.

"Good morning. How can I help you?" Nancy said with a smile.

"I'm Special Agent Odacio. I need to see the District Attorney."

"I'm afraid he's not coming in today. I can make you an appointment."

"What about Sokolov?"

"Bobby? He's with someone right now, I'm sorry."

"I can wait," Odacio said.

"It could be a while, they just sat down, and he's taking a deposition," Nancy said.

"I'll wait." And he did. While he waited, he pored over Jermaine's file again, interrupted a few times by telemarketing calls selling vacations or vehicle warranties but coming through on incoming numbers that looked local. He turned his attention to Jermaine's file. Good student, no priors. Joins the Army out of high school. He doesn't come from a military family; maybe he was patriotic, maybe he needed the free ride for school from the GI Bill. The kid wins a literary award junior year of high school, plays on the baseball team. He's on the honor list. The mother, Nellie Childs, has the restaurant. No rap sheet on the father, Reginald Raines, a steelworker. It's not a broken home… What turns a straight-laced kid like that into a bomber? Nothing in the file points to it, he thought to himself. Just then, Nancy returned.

"Bobby can see you now," she said. And motioned for Odacio to follow her into Bobby's office.

"Good morning, Agent Odacio."

"Good morning, Bobby."

"What's new in the investigation?"

"A print story in the Daily *Freeman*."

"I saw that."

"What do you think?" Odacio asked.

"What do you mean?" Bobby asked.

"Where did it come from?"

"Sonia Gonzales. It's her beat,"

"Not what I mean, Bobby," Odacio said with a clear tone.

"What are you asking me?" Bobby said with anger on his face.

"I'm asking if you are the fucking leak!" Odacio said, raising his voice.

"I'm glad they ran that story. People need to know that American Dawn is a fascist organization and that they're responsible!" Bobby yelled back.

"Bobby, are you the fucking leak?" Odacio asked, raising his voice again.

"Sonia had it. I corroborated it!"

"Asshole! Why?"

"Because of exactly what I just fucking said. These racist, fascist pieces of shit are spewing their garbage, and people are buying into it. They need to be stopped. They need to be held accountable. Brooke and I didn't always see eye to eye, but she was an amazing person. I looked up to her, and they fucking murdered her and all those other people, and for what? This shit, it's just going too far, and that fucker in the White House is fanning the flames."

"Bobby, you put people's lives in danger! What if that defector is real, and he's out there? How long do you think he's going to be walking around before they break his legs or worse? If he exists, they're going to be trying to figure out who he is and fast. You're grieving Brooke, I get it, and so if this were personal, I'd give you a pass, but this was political for you, Bobby! And you put your politics ahead of the health and safety of innocent people!" Odacio yelled.

"Politics is personal! They hate me because I'm Jewish. They hate my mother because she's Jewish. They deny the Holocaust ever happened. They tell people to go back where they come from. They spew hate in every direction, at any person who didn't come from where they came from or doesn't think like they think. Is this the world you want to live in, Odacio?" Bobby demanded.

"No. It's not, Bobby," Odacio said, settling down. "But you've made things worse for us and better for them. I don't know what we're going to find. I think American Dawn did this, but I don't know for sure. There's another suspect. If it turns out they didn't do it, and someone tried to pin it on American Dawn, it's not just going to be Brody who was a martyr. It's going to be the whole damn organization. This could be the best thing that ever happened to them."

Before Bobby responded, Odacio's phone alerted him to a text message from Kristen. It read "EMERGENCY. COME HOME OR CALL ASAP." He got up to his feet. "I've got to go."

Odacio ran through the DA's office, out the door, and to the Cherokee. As he was running, he dialed Kristen. Ring. "Answer!" Ring. "Answer!" Her voice came on. He was driving now, fast."You've reached Kristen Odacio. I'm not…"

He was thinking to himself: "Hang up! Dial again!" Same outcome. Once more. The same outcome again. "Fuck! Calm down and think," he said to himself. "Dial Bonner," he reached into his pocket, grabbed the business card. He swerved, passing another car. He was doing ninety on a residential street. "Slow down to eighty before you dial," he thought to himself. It rang twice.

'This is Bonner."

"Bonner, it's Odacio!"

"Yeah, Scout?"

"Is your man on my street?"

"Not until 1 p.m. But 'round the clock from there."

"Something's wrong. It's Kristen. It's an emergency."

"Your house?" Bonner said.

"Yeah. I'm five minutes away," Odacio said.

"I'm sending the cavalry. They'll be right on your tail."

Odacio kept driving, passing cars whenever he could, narrowly avoiding accidents. He hit the final straightaway, a two-mile stretch, hearing sirens in the background, close. He took the Cherokee to max speed, coming to a screeching halt in front of their house instead of pulling into the driveway. He got out of the car, leaving the door open in full stride, gun drawn. Approaching the front door, he realized he didn't have his keys. Instinct took over; he kicked down the door with a loud crash. Kristen yelled, "What the fuck?" She ran across the room to grab the handgun they kept locked up but didn't have the keys on her.

Odacio came through and saw her. "Where are they?" he panted, scanning the room with his gun drawn.

"What the fuck is going on?" Kirsten yelled.

"You tell me, Kristen!"

"What was the crash sound?"

"It was me coming in."

"What?" she yelled.

"I had to kick the door down!" he said.

"What the fuck did you do that for?" she screamed.

"What's going on? Your text!"

"Frank is sick!" she yelled.

"What?"

"Frank is sick! He's out back. We need to do something."

"Holy fuck, Kristen, you scared the shit out of me. Don't do that!"

"But he's really sick. We need to take him to the vet right now!"

"Let's go," Odacio said, still in a state of shock and not entirely sure what was going on. They ran out the back door. Frank was lying on his side, moaning, looking really bad. "I'll pick him up. Let's take the Cherokee; it'll be more comfortable for him," Odacio said. Frank was a big dog, not easy to carry, but he got him up into his arms. "Let's go out the side. It's a straighter shot to where I parked." As they approached the fence gate, it was open. "Why did you leave the gate open, Kristen? Christ, he could have gotten out!"

"I didn't touch the gate!" she yelled back at him. As they passed through, they stopped dead in their tracks as four troopers with guns drawn were advancing towards them from the road.

"Put the dog down, sir! ON YOUR KNEES!" one yelled.

"BOTH OF YOU! Down on the ground!" another yelled louder. Kristen immediately dropped, but Odacio was still frozen.

"I'll shoot you and the dog, you son of a bitch, get down now!"

"Honey, get down!" Kristen said. He did, gingerly placing Frank down and getting on his hands and knees.

"Officer Schmidt, clear the house!" the commanding officer yelled. He then turned to Chris and Kristen. "Is there anyone in the house?"

"No. We're the only ones here," Kristen said. "We're the homeowners. This is my husband, and that is our dog. Can you tell me what is going on?"

"I'd like to ask you the same question." The officer responded.

"I'm Special Agent Odacio, FBI. I think I can explain."

Frank was in the back seat, moaning worse than before. Odacio was swerving and passing cars in much the same manner as when he was on his way to their house, only this time, on the way to the vet. He hadn't had a chance for an emotional reaction or really even to process the state that Frank was in.

His adrenaline was still pumping. Neither he nor Kristen spoke as they sped towards the clinic. They pulled up right out front of the entrance, and Odacio carried Frank in

"How long has he been like this?" the vet asked.

"At least two hours," Kristen said.

"You should have brought him in sooner."

"We got held up," Odacio said.

"Stay in the waiting room; we'll do everything we can," the vet said. As they grabbed seats, Odacio felt a sudden rush, a wave of emotion. He put his head in his hands, maybe crying, and Kristen leaned in to console him.

"What happened?" he asked.

"I don't know. I went to the grocery store. I got everything in the cart and then realized I didn't have my card or cash on me. I turned around and came home. I couldn't have been gone more than an hour or so. I saw Frank through the kitchen window, and he didn't look right. He was moaning just like you saw. That's when I texted you."

"Kristen, I dialed you four or five times. You didn't answer."

"Yeah, I came back in to text you but left my phone on the table when I went back outside to sit with him. He needed someone to be with him. What possessed you to show up with the entire state police force?"

"Kristen, you said it was an emergency in all caps and then didn't answer your phone. I thought you were dead or being raped!"

"Honey, I love you, and I think you're amazing, but I'd probably call 911 if someone were trying to rape or murder me. I'd assume they'd get there faster."

"Jesus, Kristen. Don't send me a text like that again."

"I think you overreacted. I wrote come home or call asap.

87

Emphasis on *or call.* It's not like I'd say, hey honey, a murderer is chasing me around the house, give me a call ASAP."

"Come on!" Odacio responded.

"I'm just saying, don't go freaking out like that again."

"You know what, let's not talk. I'm going to sit and pray for Frank," Odacio said. They sat quietly for about fifteen minutes and then got called in to see the vet. They were led into an office expecting to see Frank and the vet, but it was just them. Two minutes later, the vet walked in.

"How's he doing, Doc?" Odacio asked.

"I'm afraid he didn't make it," the vet said.

"What? What do you mean?" Odacio stammered as his eyes teared up, Kristen grabbing his hand.

"There was nothing I could do to save Frank. I could only mitigate the pain. I did, and he slipped away peacefully and quickly."

Odacio, voice breaking, said, "Was it because he was too fat?" The vet looked him in the eyes and put his hands on Odacio's shoulders.

"Now, what gave you that idea, son? Frank was normal-sized for a Lab. He weighed only a pound more than he did last time I saw him. This is not your fault."

"Well, if it wasn't his weight, then what was it?" Odacio asked.

"He ingested something he shouldn't have eaten. His stomach swelled and ruptured."

"What was it? What did he eat?"

"I would need to do an autopsy to know for sure."

"Is there even such a thing as a dog autopsy?" Odacio asked.

"There is. It would take a week or two to know anything conclusive."

"Do it," Odacio said.

"Are you sure?" the vet asked.

"Yeah, just do it," he reiterated. They said goodbye and made their way back to the Cherokee, and headed home. On the car ride back, they mostly didn't talk. Odacio was going over things in his head. He began grimacing in pain. Noticeably.

"It'll be okay, Chris. Frank's in a better place now," Kristen said.

"It's not that," Odacio said.

"What is it?"

"It's my mouth. The pain is excruciating. I think it's been there all day, and I just kind of didn't notice it with all the excitement and emotion. It hurts so much. I need a pain killer, not just an Advil."

"I didn't finish my prescription for oxy. I have enough left; you can take it as soon as we get home. And I'm making an appointment with Dr. Kat right now." She pulled out her phone and dialed. "Yes. Hello. I'd like to make an appointment for my husband." She waited as the person responded. "No. Honestly, today would be ideal. He can't wait until next week." Pause. "Tomorrow morning? That would be great if that's the best you can do," she said, pausing again. "Well, we don't know what's wrong exactly. He's in a lot of pain; one of his co-workers beat him up."

When they pulled into the driveway, Kristen was driving. They had pulled over and switched as Odacio was in too much pain. She pulled to a stop. He didn't move. "Let's go," she said.

"You go ahead. I need a minute," Odacio said. "I'll be right behind you." She got out and walked through the front door, stepping over it, to get into the house. Then lifting it and kind of fitting it back into place. Odacio turned and looked over his shoulder and noticed an unmarked car, one of Bonner's men, parked about a hundred feet past the driveway. He got out of the car and walked toward the side of the house, and stared at the open gate. Thirty seconds passed. He was still staring. He pulled his phone out of his pocket, hit the recent calls button, and clicked Bonner's number.

"This is Bonner."

"It's Odacio. Before you say anything, *anything at all*, I don't want to hear it. I'm sure those boys had a field day and are laughing their asses off at my expense, but I'm in excruciating pain; I've got no front door, my dog is dead, and I'm not in the mood to be made fun of."

"Roger that. I'm sorry about your dog."

"I'm holding it together, but here's the thing. He was fine when I left this morning. He was out back in the yard. Someone came in through the gate while Kristen was out and poisoned Frank. They left the gate open. I've got half a mind to go to Keith's trailer and rip his Adam's apple from his throat and then begin torturing him. But I'm in too much pain to do that right now," Odacio said.

"You mean like emotional?"

"No….. well yes…. but no. I think you broke my jaw or something. I'm going to the dentist first thing in the morning. I need you to escort Kristen to work tomorrow, just see that she gets there alright."

"Of course, Scout. What time should I pick her up?"

"No. I just want you to follow her. I don't want her to know she's being escorted," Odacio said.

"That's stupid. Why don't you just tell her what's going on?" Bonner asked.

"It's been a really long day. I'm not 100% sure about the dog.

I'm like 90% sure. But I've just had a shit day, and I'm not up to having the conversation right now. What I'm asking you to do is follow her, don't let her know you're following her, and just watch her walk into the nursing home. That's all. Can you do that for me?"

"I really think you can tell her about this. She can handle it. She's tough."

"I know she's tough!" Odacio snapped, but kind of under his breath so that Kristen didn't hear from inside. "I married her. That's beside the point right now. I'll tell her but not today. You broke my jaw in a drunken rage. All I'm asking is that you follow her, don't get made, and watch her walk in the nursing home. Then we'll be square. Is that too much to ask?"

"Okay, fair enough," Bonner said as they both hung up.

12

Chapter 12

In the morning, Odacio woke up in pain, but not the worst of it, as the oxy was keeping it manageable. Kristen was getting ready for work. He had slept in later than normal on account of the drugs. She noticed he was awake and talked to him from the ensuite bathroom as he lay in bed.

"How you doing, sweetie? How's the pain?"

"It's okay," he said.

"Jackie called for you earlier; you didn't hear it ring. I picked up."

"What did he say?"

"Grace is doing great, and he's looking forward to spending more time with the grandkids."

"Did he have a message?" he asked.

"No. I told him you were out of commission for at least a few hours. I told him about Frank and about how Bonner was beating you up."

"You're kidding me, right? Tell me you are fucking with me," he said.

"Well, I didn't say it exactly like that."

"What did you say exactly?"

"I don't know, does it really matter?"

"Stop saying that. It didn't happen. I have a lot going on right now, and I'm on edge, and I don't need you going around town telling people, especially my boss, that Bonner is beating me up!"

"Okay, I hear you. I won't say that again. But.."

"What? But what?" he asked.

"I may have mentioned it to your mother too."

"What?"

"She called again. You never called her back."

"Kristen!"

"I told you to call her. If you had done so, this never would have happened."

"No. If you didn't tell her, it never would have happened!"

"Let's change the subject," she said. "I confirmed with Jack and Donna. We're going over there at 8 p.m. on Saturday. I wasn't sure if you'd be able to eat solid foods, so I said after dinner. Oh…"

"No. Kristen. You didn't. You know what? Don't even say anything."

"You should get up and get ready. I'm sorry I can't drive you. I've got to run." She walked over, kissed him goodbye, and moved quickly downstairs. From the window, he watched her pull out of the driveway and leave. About twenty seconds later, he saw Bonner drive-by, following her, as planned. Odacio got ready and headed out to the dentist's office.

Bonner kept a few hundred yards back from Kristen as he followed her, always trying to keep one car between them for cover. Within just a few minutes, he was sure no one else followed her and was just going through the motions. He wouldn't usually take a call when tailing someone, but the coast seemed clear, and it was a local number he didn't recognize, making him think it could be germane to the case, so he answered.

"This is Bonner."

"Mr. Bonner?"

"Yeah, speaking."

"This is Jared, and I'm calling because we know you're the type of person who loves to go on vacation to warm sunny places, and we can offer that to you today, free of charge."

"A free vacation?" Bonner said skeptically.

"Yessir. All expenses paid, besides airfare, and all we need you to do is go to an informational session about other great offers, many of them free as well."

"Son, how did you get this number?"

"We got it from a list of people who love free vacations. That describes you, am I right, sir?"

"I know you got my number from a list. I want to know where you got it in the first place. I am a Senior Investigator with the state police, and I am on the DNC list. That stands for do not call. Do you copy?"

"I'm sorry, sir, there must have been some mistake. We thought you were someone who enjoyed free vacations to warm sunny places, but maybe it is your wife we are looking for."

"You'll need to look pretty hard then because she doesn't exist!"

"I'm sorry to hear that sir, let me just say we can add something extra special to this offer right now if you are willing to commit today. It's free. All we need is a valid credit card number to hold the reservation. You can decide on location and dates whenever you like."

Bonner hung up with some force. "Fuck," he said aloud to himself. In the back and forth, he realized he had made an error with his attention divided. He thought he was a car back from Kristen, but he was right behind her, and they were at a red light. "Fuck! Don't look back, don't look back," he said aloud, but they locked eyes in her mirror. "Shit! Don't get out of the car, don't get out of the car." Her door opened, and her left leg came out first. Bonner, panicking, got out of the car quickly and put his hands up and palms up at his side, looking like a kid with his hand caught in the cookie jar but ineffectively feigning innocence. She was out of the car now, too, walking towards him with an angry look on her face. Bonner's mind was racing to try to think of a cover story, but nothing was coming to him. He had a thing for Kristen, she reminded him of someone, and he wasn't thinking straight.

"Okay, okay," he began. "I know what this looks like. And... I know it looks like I'm stalking you, but that is not what is happening here." It was the best he could do.

"Stalking me? What?" she said, trying to process that.

"No. No. Believe me. It's not that. I know it looks like that. But I'm not stalking you," he repeated.

"Wait, a second! Are you stalking me?"

"No. That's what I'm trying to tell you. I am not stalking you now. I mean, I've never stalked you, and I never will stalk you. This is all just a big coincidence," he said.

"I assumed it was a coincidence, but now I think you *are* stalking me."

"Kristen, nothing could be further from the truth. I was just... I was just driving because, well, I had to go to the nursing home because there was an emergency there."

"An emergency at the nursing home? What happened? I'm going there now!" Fuck, he thought to himself, another misstep.

"No. No. It's fine. It's not at the nursing home. It's near the nursing home. So I knew that I had to go towards the nursing home because it was near the nursing home. Where the emergency was."

"What is the emergency?"

"It's all fine now. It's being handled. It was a false alarm." Fuck. Another misstep, he thought to himself. That was his ticket out of the situation, and he just discarded it.

"Okay. So you're not stalking me, and there's no emergency? Those are the two things I need to know about this situation where we bumped into each other?" she said.

"Exactly. Nothing more and nothing less," Bonner said.

"Well. You've got some nerve. Who do you think you are?"

"What? I'm sorry?"

"You've been beating my husband! What's wrong with you?'

"Wait a minute, no… you see… You've got it wrong again."

"What do you mean I've got it wrong?" she asked.

"Um. Well. You see, it's like this…."

"Did he attack you?" Silence, a dazed look on his face. "Did. He. Attack. You?"

"Um. Unfortunately. Let's just say it was self-defense and leave it at that."

"I can't believe this. That bastard! I've been feeling bad for him. Are you okay?"

"Oh yes. Now. I'm definitely okay. It's in the past. What's done is done. There's no unfinished business. It's behind us," he said.

"No wonder he wouldn't let me call his union rep. Brett, you promise me, If he lays a hand on you again, you call me immediately!"

Odacio was in the chair in the dentist's office. They had examined him and taken the x-rays already. He was waiting on a diagnosis, scrolling ESPN to pass the time. Dr. Kat came back in. He was in his fifties, tall and slender, and looked like a runner. He had an upper-class British accent.

"I'm afraid I don't have good news, Chris."

"Just give it to me."

"Very well. You've got cracks in three contiguous teeth. We're going to need to do root canals on all three."

"Jesus! Three root canals?" Odacio asked.

"I'm going to need back up from a colleague. Three in a row is a lot, and it's somewhat of a challenge."

"Are you serious?" he said.

"Christopher, I could not be more serious. We have no other choice. You must understand; you may have a hard time eating."

"For how long?"

"A week or so, maybe longer."

"What am I going to eat?"

"A lot of liquids. Maybe some oatmeal. A lot of oatmeal."

"How long will it take to do?" he asked.

"Oh, you will need to clear your schedule for the rest of the day."

"Goddammit."

"Also, and this is very important. Your jaw is going to pop out of place from time to time. You will need Kristen or someone to jerk it back into place immediately. I will show you what I mean by demonstrating on one of the assistants," Dr. Kat said.

"Not required. I'm familiar with it," Odacio said.

"It will hurt every time, but I am afraid there is not another option. There's one more thing, and this is even more important."

"Ok. Tell me."

"You must stop getting punched in the face. Do whatever you need to do to put distance between you and your abuser. This man, who is it? This, Bonner? You must avoid Bonner. Your dental health depends upon it."

"Yeah. Okay," Odacio said.

"Now. I will go make all the necessary preparations." Dr. Kat exited the room.

Odacio laid in the chair, staring up at the ceiling. Thirty minutes passed by. One of the assistants was walking by the door, and he called out to make sure they hadn't forgotten about him. "Dr. Kat will be in shortly," she told him. Then his phone rang. It was, of course, Bonner.

"Please tell me everything is fine and that she got there safely. I can't take any more bad news right now," Odacio said.

"Well, yes, she's fine, Scout," Bonner said.

"Okay, so everything went according to plan?"

"Not exactly."

"Not exactly, how?"

"On account of, well, I screwed up."

"And…"

"Well, she saw me," Bonner said.

"How do you know?"

"Because we talked about it."

"What?"

"She got out of the car, and we had a conversation. But don't worry, I covered it up all good. She doesn't suspect anything," Bonner said.

"Well, I guess that's okay then. All's well that ends well."

"Yeah. But there's one thing. Now, I was thinking on my feet, and I didn't want her to think for one second that you had sent me to tail her. Like you said, it's your business when you do or don't tell her something like that. So I covered your butt well. But in the process, these things are delicate you gotta recognize, she may have come away with the impression that you started it."

"Started what?" Odacio asked.

"The fights."

"What!?"

"Now you've gotta stick with that, or the whole story will come crashing down, and you'll be exposed," Bonner said.

"What did you tell her?"

"I don't even remember. It was all so fast, and I was doing mental gymnastics to keep your secret safe. The important thing is that you stick to the story for both our sakes."

"What story?" Odacio asked.

"That what I did, I did in self-defense. That's all."

"Bonner, no. I'm not doing that."

"No. No. No. I didn't want to have to do this, but Scout, I am going to invoke man code," Bonner said.

'What?"

"You know, guy code, man code, whatever you want to call it." At that moment, Dr. Kat came back into the room.

"Christopher, who are you talking to?" Dr. Kat asked.

"Hold on," Odacio said as he heard Bonner say something about Fawlty Towers.

"No," Dr. Kat said. "Are you talking to Bonner? Hang up at once, or we'll cancel the entire procedure!"

"Bonner, I've got to go."

99

Odacio still had the effects of novocaine and would for a few hours. He drove himself home, getting back a lot later than planned. Kristen had already done her full eight-hour shift and was home in the kitchen waiting for him when he arrived, and she did not look happy.

"Do you have anything you want to tell me?" She asked.

"It didn't go so well. I'm good for now, but I need to go back in a couple of weeks," he said. He had that novocaine lisp and drooled a little while he spoke.

"Not about that. I want the truth about what happened. Between you and Brett," she said.

"Let's just forget about it. It's water under the bridge."

"How dare you?" she said.

"How dare I what?" he said, trying to fight the lisp, realizing he sounded ridiculous.

"How dare you attack an old man like that?"

"Bonner's not an old man, Kristen; he's a 60 something-year-old monster!"

13

Chapter 13

Odacio woke feeling well enough to run, so he did. When he approached the trail, he headed west instead of east like he normally would with Frank. East would have brought him to the cement ruins, but west took him to an old railroad trestle. The trestle connected two ridges over a creek with a nice view, but it was in disrepair, and people weren't supposed to walk on it. They did, but it was too dangerous for Frank. Odacio didn't want to go to the trestle so much as run away from where he would have gone with Frank. After the run, he came in to meet Kristen for coffee. He kissed her good morning and sat down.

"You look in better spirits," she said.

"It's like night and day. I feel amazing, in contrast," he said.

"Good."

"You sleep well?"

"Yeah. Look, we didn't finish our conversation last night. I don't want to harp on it, but I don't want it to go unresolved either," she said.

"Okay. I'll tell you what happened. And then hopefully we

can put it to bed."

"Thanks," she said.

"I started it. The first night. We each hit each other once, then we both came to our senses. The second night it was an accident. He got into it with Fin, I was trying to defuse it, and he clocked me accidentally. That's the whole truth."

"I appreciate you leveling with me. It's surprising because he seems like a nice guy."

"He's not a nice guy, Kristen. He can be a fun guy, a funny guy. But he's not a *nice* guy, particularly when he drinks. He's got a problem."

"I think I can read people. Underneath, if you got to know him, I think you'd like him," she said.

"Ha, well, I don't think *you* would."

"What does that mean?" she asked.

"I think he would offend your sensibilities."

"And which sensibilities are those?" she asked.

"The liberal ones."

"I'm not a moron. I can read people. I think maybe there's more there than you're allowing for. Have you thought about talking to him about his drinking?"

"I'm not his mother. But yeah, I did say something."

"How'd he react?"

"He told me I wasn't his mother and changed the subject," he said.

"Well, maybe you could try a little harder."

"I think it's a relapse. Whatever problem he has, he's solved it before."

"What makes you think that?"

"Fin basically said as much. Not long before Bonner tried to floor him."

"Well, I think there's more to him than what we see."

"I guess that's true of everyone." Odacio finished his coffee. "Can I drive you to work this morning?"

"If you're able to pick me up at five."

"Sure." Odacio showered quickly. While waiting for Kristen, he grabbed his cell and headed out to the front porch, opening the front door, which was still off its hinges. He had forgotten about that with everything going on. He took a seat on one of the deck chairs and dialed Jackie.

"Good morning, Scout."

"Good morning, sir. American Dawn raised the stakes yesterday."

"How so?" Jackie asked.

"They came to my house when we were out and poisoned Frank."

"Is he ok?"

"Not at all. He's dead."

"I'm sorry to hear that, Scout, that's terrible. How do you know he was poisoned?" Jackie asked.

"I don't know for sure. But the evidence suggests it. I'm getting an autopsy done. In the meantime, it's safer to assume that it was what it looks like."

"Agreed. Are you taking precautions?"

"Yes. Bonner's got someone watching the house 24-7, and I'm driving Kristen to and from work."

"Good. We need to talk about her."

"Kristen?" Odacio asked.

"Yeah. Her name has shown up on the American Dawn message boards."

"Motherfuckers."

"We pinpointed the source. It came from an IP address at the

Kole County Library. There were seven people signed in at the time. But they don't sign them into a specific computer. One of those seven was a kid doing homework or something. We're looking into the other six."

"Give me the list."

"Negative. I'm going to handle it," Jackie said.

"What's the nature of the threat?"

"Most of it was just bluster. The most specific was something like 'We should give her what's coming to her too.'"

"I want to fry these guys, sir. American Dawn is meeting is on Saturday evening. Can we wire the barn and listen in?" Odacio asked.

"I doubt it. I'm sorry. You might have missed this yesterday, but they're doing a rally outside the county building this afternoon, in response to the *Freeman* article."

"What time?"

"4 p.m. I've decided to assign a few agents to work the crowd. They'll be circulating petitions about second amendment rights to collect the names of people in attendance. They're going to try to focus on the organizers. We'll check the list to see if any of them have criminal records."

"I appreciate it, sir. Did something change that made you come around on American Dawn?"

"No. The organization may be involved or even responsible. I just think you're giving them too much credence compared to other possibilities."

"Okay. I'll be there too."

"Good. It's shaping up to be big. They have 1000 RSVP's on their page. Attendance will be a lot lower than that, but it's shaping up to be their largest rally to date. They're milking that story for all it's worth. The bump they got from Brody Wilcox is looking like it's going to be outdone by this new boost from that article," Jackie said.

"Let's catch up on a few other things," Odacio said. "I wanted to talk about Wilcox, but any updates on the Brooke list or the our Farkus phone?"

"The what?"

"The Sydney Farkus phone."

"On Farkus, his son Max has been paying the bill. We think he has the phone. He's out of the country on business but back Monday. We'll know more then. We're also working with Verizon to pinpoint the location when the call was made. The Brooke list alibis are all checking out so far. I think that's a dead end."

"Alright. So I paid a visit to Wilcox in county. It was interesting."

"How so?"

"First, he doesn't buy into the politics. He doesn't care about it. He says they used him and that he's got nothing to do with the cause. It wasn't what I expected. He also said that he heard chatter about them targeting a Mexican taco shop, but he wouldn't say who from."

"How recent? He's been in county a while."

"I should have asked, but I guess we can assume it was before February when he was arrested. He said he'd give us names if we could get him moved to minimum security to serve out his sentence."

"He hasn't been sentenced yet."

"Yeah, but it's imminent. He's taking a plea."

"I'm not inclined towards it, Scout, for the obvious reasons."

"What if this is the first in a string of bombings, sir? Wilcox might be able to help us cut that off at the pass."

"He'll tell you anything you want to hear and send you on a wild goose chase. And you said yourself he's recounting a conversation that happened months ago."

"Okay. I'll take another run at him and see what he'll tell me without a deal. Maybe we can give it a second consideration at that point?"

"Fine. Do you have anything new on Jermaine?" Jackie asked.

"Not yet. We're going to re-interview him today or tomorrow."

"He's your hot lead at the moment. At the risk of sounding like a broken record, I'm concerned you're only focused on leads that point to American Dawn."

"We'll go back at Jermaine, sir."

"Okay, is there anything else?" Jackie asked.

"Yeah. I know you think it'll be difficult to get a wiretap to listen in on the American Dawn meeting, but I think we should try. Even if they aren't good for the bomb, they've now poisoned my dog and threatened my wife."

"Okay, I'll give it a try. I'll be in touch later this morning."

Kristen came out the back door and walked around the house. She spun her finger in the air, signaling she was ready. They hopped in the Cherokee and pulled out of the driveway.

"Can we talk?" Odacio asked.

"Of course. What's wrong?"

"We need to be extra careful. I need you to be really aware of your surroundings. I want to drive you to and from work everyday for now," he said.

"What's going on?"

"American Dawn. I don't know if they're responsible for the bomb. It could be a smokescreen. Jackie and I have different views on it, but we agree they're not good people. I think they

106

poisoned Frank."

"What?"

"The gate was open. You didn't open it. Someone came in."

"That could be a coincidence. Maybe one of us left it open and forgot," she said.

"I would think that, but Jackie's been monitoring the message boards. They posted our address and names."

"Seriously?" she asked.

"Bonner's got a man posted a hundred feet from the house 24-7."

"Wait. Was that what that was about? Was Bonner following me?"

"Yeah. I asked him to," Odacio said.

"That's a relief. I thought he was stalking me. But I don't appreciate that. You should have told me."

"You just said you thought a man was stalking you, and you didn't tell me."

"I didn't know for sure."

"Neither did I," he retorted.

"Fine. Let's move on."

"Are you scared?" Odacio asked.

"No," she said confidently.

"You should be. It's helpful in a situation like this. I'd feel better if you were at least nervous. Be on alert. Don't go to lunch alone; order for delivery. Eat inside the nursing home. Think about every move you make and think through the lens of whether it's safe or not. Just for the next few days while we figure out what's going on."

Odacio pulled up in front of the nursing home, kissed Kristen goodbye, and watched her walk in. He checked his phone before pulling out. He had a text message from Bonner telling him to meet up at his office at the State Police Headquarters instead of the deli. It was a short drive. Odacio walked in and approached the desk officer. "I'm Special Agent Odacio, here to see Bonner."

"We met the other day. Go right in. It's the third door on the right."

"Good morning," Bonner said as Odacio sat down. Bonner's office was bare. There was a mostly empty bookshelf and a window with a view of the parking lot. There was one picture frame on his desk, but it was lying flat, face down.

"What's new?" Odacio asked.

"American Dawn rally at 4 p.m.," Bonner said.

"Yup. I'm going."

"We'll be covering security. Separating the counter-protestors, if there any," Bonner said.

"What else?"

"I held off on Jermaine while you were out. I figured we'd do that together and that he ain't going nowhere. I called him just now to schedule a second interview, but he's not around. Said he's visiting his father out of town. It was a strange conversation."

"How so?" Odacio asked.

"He sounded almost like he was disappointed that he wasn't available. As if he wanted to meet again."

"Could be he wants to know what we're thinking and who we're looking at, to get a read and see if we're on his scent yet."

"Yeah. Most likely."

"There's the other possibility as well, that he just had nothing to do with it. You read his file. He played baseball, was on the honor roll. Nothing indicates that he was into drugs. Maybe the Conejos were accidental. They easily could have had business there, and the person was late, or maybe they were just hungry," Odacio said.

"I don't know if we're dealing with a Lex Luther level criminal mastermind or just some set of weird coincidences. The simplest solution I can think of is Jermaine has some reason to get a Conejo or Brooke and sets up the American Dawn thing to divert our attention."

"Yeah, but the American Dawn angle was brilliant if that's what it was. Would that same brilliant person not assume we'd look up his military record and see his specialty?" Odacio asked.

"You're right; that doesn't add up. Anything new on the 'Our Farkus' phone?"

"The son, Max, has been paying the bill. He's out of the country until Monday. We'll be able to identify the radius the call originated from as well."

"What else?"

"I told you that Jackie's been monitoring the chatter on American Dawn message boards. Now there's a threat associated with Kristen."

"Those motherfuckers," Bonner said.

"Someone in American Dawn figured out she's my wife. They've named her as a target as well, and there have been several posts about it."

"They've crossed a red line. The gloves are off," Bonner said.

"You're telling me."

"We need to cut it off at the pass."

"How do you mean?" Odacio asked.

"By figuring out what they're cooking up before it comes out of the oven."

"I asked Jackie if he could get us a wire inside the Browns' barn so that we could monitor the meeting on Saturday," Odacio said.

"That would be a good start."

"Yeah, but he doesn't think it's likely," Odacio began. "He's making calls; I expect to hear back from him later today. It would be hard to get it inside without them noticing between today and tomorrow."

"Maybe not. We know where both of them are going to be at 4 p.m. today; they ain't got no butlers or anything like that."

"So we'd need a green light by around three at the very latest to make the logistics work. And we'd need a locksmith on-site with us."

"Not necessarily. It'd be easy enough and pretty quick to drill small holes from the outside wall and push the bug right through. It would be so small; they'd never notice it," Bonner said.

"Speaking of…," Odacio looked down at his phone. "It's Jackie. I'm going to put him on speaker," he said. "Sir. I'm here with Bonner. He's fully briefed."

"Pleasure to meet you," Jackie said.

"And you as well, sir," Bonner responded.

"I wish I had better news to share. No-go on the warrant for that tap. I'm sorry."

"Thank you for trying, sir."

"ASAC, there's gotta be an angle here," Bonner said.

"Give me something, and I'll work it. But I need something more than we have now."

"What's your lead time?" Bonner asked.

"Hard to say. Without an imminent threat, it might be hard to get a fast turnaround under any circumstance."

"We need a fast turnaround. A woman's life has been

threatened," Bonner said.

"I know that woman. She's like a goddaughter to me. But the threat isn't specific or imminent."

"Okay, let's see if we can't think of something. We'll call you back," Bonner said.

"I'm standing by," Jackie said before hanging up.

"So much for that," Odacio said.

"Don't give up so fast."

"You got an idea?"

"No. But we need to think. I can't abide by this." Bonner paused and stared out the window for ten long seconds. "These fuckers want to fight dirty? I can fight dirty."

"What are you thinking?"

"I'm saying fuck the warrant. I can just go over to Keith's house a little before 4 p.m, drill the holes and put a tap in there," Bonner said.

"Setting aside that it's illegal for a minute, anything that came from it would be inadmissible."

"At this moment, we're not trying to build a case. We're trying to prevent a crime. Against your wife."

"There's gotta be another way," Odacio said. "We need more time."

"That's one thing we can't get more of."

"Come on, let's think. There's gotta be an angle." They stared out the window again and sat in silence for two minutes, maybe longer.

"Okay," Bonner began. "Maybe I have something. Come round my side of the desk. Bring the chair." Odacio did. Bonner pulled up American Dawn's website. "Take a look at this site, Odacio. What do you see?"

"A contribution link everywhere I look."

"Okay, humor them. Click through. Now, what do you see?"

"I see amounts. It looks like they're steering me towards $100."

"What else?"

"I don't know. It's tax-deductible."

"Okay. Put $100 in there and click through." Bonner instructed him. "Okay, now, what are you looking at?"

"The ways I can fulfill the pledge."

"And what are those?"

"Well, I can do it via credit card, or I can send a check to Keith's address."

"And who is that check made out to?"

"American Dawn, LLC," Odacio said.

"Come on, Scout, it's right under your nose." Odacio stared at the screen.

"Holy shit. An LLC isn't tax-deductible! Contributions to American Dawn are not tax-deductible!" Odacio said, pounding the table with his fist.

"Not last time I checked. That stupid son of a bitch is breaking the law and probably doesn't even know it!"

"Brilliant, Bonner. What made you think of this?" Odacio asked.

"I considered contributing at one point. I noticed this and decided not to. I didn't think about it again until now."

"Seriously? You were going to contribute to these fuckers?" Odacio sounded exasperated.

"Never mind that. Get ASAC Jackie back on the line." Odacio dialed.

"Sir, we've got an angle."

"Give it to me, Scout," Jackie said. Odacio paused, annoyed that Jackie called him Scout in front of Bonner.

"You're on speaker again, sir. American Dawn's website is soliciting tax-deductible contributions to an LLC."

"Well, those contributions aren't tax-deductible at all."

"No, sir," Odacio said, smiling, he and Bonner giving each other a high five.

"That's enough to get that warrant, but I don't think it would be fast-tracked given the nature of the crime," Jackie said as Bonner picked something up off his desk and threw it across the room; it shattered on the wall. He got up immediately and picked a piece of it up, and put it in his pocket, carefully avoiding the shattered glass. It was the picture in the picture frame Odacio assumed.

"Really, sir, no old favors you can call in?"

"I'm afraid not. The best I can do on that is executable on Monday."

"We'll take it anyway. Have the boys ready with their fishing poles."

"Sounds good. Keep in communication," Jackie said before hanging up.

"Now what?" Bonner asked as he stared out the window.

"Let's get tacos. It feels like days since I've eaten anything solid," Odacio said.

Odacio and Bonner waited at the counter until their food came up, then took it back to the table. Bonner took the seat facing the door. Odacio sat down across from him.

"This is authentic Mexican, not the gringo stuff," Bonner said.

"You been there?" Odacio asked.

"Once. About ten years back. Near Cancun. I spent most of the time making my way down the coast. Visiting the smaller towns. There was one, Tulum; I highly recommend it."

"Funny. You strike me as someone who would stay put in the tourist area."

"That's right. The woman I was with, actually Kristen reminds me of her; she planned it. I just did what she told me, went where she told me. You know how it is," Bonner said.

"Yeah."

"It kind of broadened my horizons, you might say. Before that, I thought Mexican food was Taco Bell. I don't know; sometimes, a situation you're in impacts how you think and experience things. I tell you, if I went there alone and went down that coast myself, I probably would've hated it. The first shit I took, throwing the toilet paper in the basket. Hell. I would have booked the next flight back."

"What? You can't flush toilet paper there?"

"No. Not outside the tourist areas."

"That would throw me for a loop."

"They're good people, I guess. The Mexicans. They work hard," Bonner said.

"Most immigrants here are too. A lot of them didn't have it as easy as we did growing up."

"Some maybe. Others not so much. You come to this country and go on welfare? That's a bridge too far for me."

"That doesn't happen as often as you might think," Odacio said.

"But it does happen."

"Yeah. It does."

"It don't bother you none?"

"I guess I don't think about it much," Odacio said.

"Like being Cuban?" Bonner asked.

"What?" Odacio said.

"You said that to me. Your father was Cuban, but you don't

114

think about it much."

"Yeah. I grew up with my mother. He died when I was young."

"Was he a defector from Castro?"

"I don't really know much about him. He worked in the State Department or something. My mother wouldn't really talk about him. I guess I grew up looking and feeling white. I can thank him for the fluency in Spanish, though; it comes in handy."

"More and more every year. They're taking the jobs our boys won't do anymore. It's a shame, really," Bonner said.

"How do you mean?"

"Our boys, they grow up on these computers. Not learning what real work is. It has an effect. It changes the character. Then on top of that, you got people with the brains and means to go to college and the people who don't. It used to be you could make a good living without going to college. Now you got no choice whether you belong there or not."

"Yeah. I can see that."

"What about Kristen? What's her maiden name?"

"McNamara."

"I thought so. I like Irish girls," Bonner said.

"Let's avoid that."

"Avoid what?"

"Talking about Kristen," Odacio said.

"Seriously? We should avoid talking about Kristen? I mean, we're sitting here, talking about Mexicans and Cubans, but that ain't what we're thinking about, is it?" Bonner said.

"I can think about two things at the same time."

"No, you can't. You can toggle back and forth, maybe, but that's beside the point. I think we both know what we need to do in this situation," Bonner said.

"I'm torn about it. I don't want to roll that way."

"And I don't think you should. You should stay a boy scout. I mean that" Bonner said, sounding sincere. "Stay that way as long as you can."

"What's that supposed to mean?" Odacio asked, annoyed.

"It means you've got that spark. That idea that you're going to save the world and right the wrongs. At some point, you'll be close to retirement and realize the world still needs a lot of saving and a lot of wrongs written right and that it's someone else's turn to pick up where you left off. Not to finish the job but to continue it until someone after him. You're young. Stay that way as long as you can."

"What are you getting at, Bonner?"

"What I'm getting at is if these boys are planning something regarding Kristen, I want to know what it is. And planting an illegal tap, listening in, that ain't nothing to me. Hell, I've done worse. I'm going to do it. Alone."

"Fuck that."

"It's decided," Bonner said.

"No."

"You ain't my mother, and you ain't the judge of whether I'm right or wrong. I call my own shots."

"No. As in, I'm coming with you," Odacio said.

"No way. You'd probably screw it up somehow anyway."

"I'm coming."

"Something could go wrong. I've got more experience and less to lose. It's a rational decision," Bonner said.

"Bonner, it's not a decision, and this is not a state police operation. This is a Kristen Odacio operation. I've got the jurisdiction."

"Well….Touche, I guess."

14

Chapter 14

The state police put up barricades to funnel protestors in a manner that didn't disrupt vehicular traffic more than was necessary. That meant there were only two ways in and out of the courtyard outside the county building where the rally was happening. It was only 3:20 p.m., but a crowd had already formed. About twenty men in military-like uniforms were stationed like a security force around the perimeter. They were holding guns of various sorts pointed at the ground. They were there mostly as a statement of force but also to put a scare into Antifa or any other ragtag group of counter-protesters that they thought might show. A few men with clipboards were circulating petitions.

At 3:25 p.m. Officer Schmidt surveyed the scene and saw an SUV pull up. Four more men in military-like uniforms carrying weapons filed into the courtyard, dispersing quickly in a way that looked well choreographed, not improvised. Schmidt turned to another officer, Walker, and said, "I count 24. That's three for each of us. And we're still thirty-five minutes out."

"What do you think?" Walker asked.

"I think we need back-up," Schmidt said.

"Should we radio the C.O.?" Walker asked.

"What's he going to do? It's not like there's another police force to call. We got two men out sick and two more on vacation. It's just us," Schmidt said.

"They could send in the suits. I saw them do that once." Walker noted.

Odacio was on the far side of the courtyard. He was on the lookout for Keith and Lenora Brown. When they arrived, he'd text Bonner signaling him to go ahead and plant the bug. Odacio wore sunglasses and a baseball cap, trying not to stick out and making it less likely the Browns recognized him. It wasn't that he couldn't be seen, but better if he wasn't. He was leaning up against one of the barricades.

The plan was that Bonner would park on a small road to the east of the Brown's property and make his way about a mile, through the woods on foot. This way, no nosy neighbors would take note of his sedan coming in and out of the Browns' driveway. Where Bonner was parked, it was common for cars to pull over, as there was a trail down to a lake where people fished. It added about forty minutes to the whole operation, but it was smart. Bonner was going to hole up in the woods and wait for Odacio to signal him, then he'd get to work. The one element left to chance was whether Lenora Brown would be there too, but they thought she would be.

"Sir, this is Schmidt. Things are getting pretty hairy down here. We're outgunned pretty good. Any chance you can send in back up?"

"All officers are deployed. Over."

"Talking about the suits, sir."

"Taken under advisement, Officer. Back at you soon. Out."

At 3:40 p.m., four more armed guards filed into place. The crowd was big already, easily 150 people, but Odacio didn't see the Browns yet. There were signs, lots of them. All the normal fare, many Q signs, some 'Free Brody' signs, and a few signs that read 'Fuck the Daily Freeman.' There was some skirmish on the north end of the courtyard, just beyond the barricade—a lot of yelling. Schmidt and Walker held their position, most other officers present responded. Odacio saw from afar a counter-protestor and an American Dawn demonstrator throwing punches at one another. They were separated by cops, put into two different police vehicles, and driven off to the holding cell.

"Sir, we're down to six officers in the square. Well over twenty armed guards. We're feeling outgunned here," Schmidt radioed in again.

"Hold your ground, son. I'm sorry, the request was denied. We can't spare them, over."

It was 3:50 p.m. now, and Keith Brown was within Odacio's sight, but Lenora was nowhere to be seen. "Fuck," he thought to himself. 3:52, still no sign. The rally was supposed to start in eight minutes. People were pouring in. If Lenora came in late, it would be hard for Odacio to spot her. She was tall, though, and that would help. The officers who arrested the two that got in a fight returned. The station was only a couple of minutes away, and the desk sergeant evidently didn't keep them back to fill out paperwork. Good call.

"Odacio," a voice from behind called. He glanced back. It was Sokolov.

"Bobby. This is the last place I thought I'd run into you."

"I like to know what I'm up against."

119

"Do me a favor, don't use my name. Actually, we probably shouldn't talk; I'm working," Odacio said.

"Understood. Catch you later then," Bobby said before moving about seven feet away, minding his business.

Odacio scanned the crowd again. Still no sign of Lenora. He noticed the agents with clipboards working some of the organizers near the stage. Odacio's cell phone alerted him to an incoming text from Bonner. It was just a question mark coming through on the Signal app they'd both downloaded before splitting up. Messages on Signal are encrypted and auto delete which was helpful for this operation. Odacio wrote "YELLOW," then looked up again, scanning the crowd. He spotted a tall woman on the northwest side. It was her. One minute to spare. He picked up his phone again and texted "GREEN" to Bonner, then heard yelling behind him.

Sokolov had managed to get into a fight. Instinct kicked in, Odacio tried to break it up. He ended up wrestling the other man to the ground, but it looked like Odacio was the one doing the fighting. The next thing he knew, he had cuffs on. It happened so quickly he didn't have time to show his credentials. "I'm with the FBI. The badge is in my pocket," Odacio said as they approached the cop car.

"I've gotta bring you in. We can sort it out at the station," the officer said.

Odacio had a lot going through his head. One of those things was Bonner's voice saying, 'You'd probably screw it up somehow.' He needed to give Bonner a heads up when the clock started ticking on the Browns' drive from the rally back to their house. The desk officer recognized Odacio right away, and it was clear he was going to be released, but erasing an arrest takes longer than a minute. It takes fifty-one minutes, apparently. He grabbed his things, including his cell phone, and started running back towards the rally, looking at his phone as he ran. He slowed down. The text from Bonner read FIN as in finished. That was quick. People were filing out of the courtyard by the time he got back. The Browns were among the last to leave. He'd missed the whole thing.

"Fuck!" he thought to himself, realizing he was late to pick up Kristen. He ran full speed to the Cherokee, dialing Bonner as he ran, with keys in the ignition, and was in reverse by the time Bonner picked up.

"I'm clear," Bonner said as he picked up, skipping the hello.

"Good. No hitches?"

"None."

"Let's talk about tomorrow." His phone beeped, signaling another call. "Shit. Hold on. Ten seconds." Kristen was calling. He toggled over. "I'm sorry. I'm en route, just a few minutes. Got held up."

"How long?" she asked.

"Ten minutes. I'm sorry. I'm on the other line; I've gotta jump." He toggled back. "Bonner, you there?"

"Yeah."

"So for tomorrow, what's your thinking?" Odacio asked.

"We need to be within a thousand feet of the barn to listen in. We'll approach through the woods, the same path I took today. There's a rock formation that provides good cover. We'll hole up there. The meeting's at 5 p.m.; sundown isn't until after 7 p.m., so we'll be able to make our way in fine. We might need flashlights on the way out, but even that we should try to avoid."

"I'm supposed to go with Kristen to our neighbor's house at 8 p.m. Should I cancel?"

"The meeting is posted as 5 p.m. We should get there early

121

and stay late in case there's an after meeting, but you should be able to get back in time to join her."

"Okay. I'll tell Kristen we have some research work that we need to do together."

"No, tell her we're going fishing like we're burying the hatchet or something. In case something goes wrong, we'll have a reason our cars are parked out there."

"Right," Odacio said.

"What happened at the rally, any trouble?"

"I don't think so. I missed some of it. Actually, almost all of it."

"Why?"

"I got arrested. I was trying to break up a fight, and it looked like I was part of it. Apparently, someone else was trying to beat the communism out of Sokolov."

"You should have let that happen," Bonner said.

"I thought you might say that."

"No. Listen to me. I'd like to see Sokolov get whooped, but that's not what I'm talking about. I'm talking about focusing on our prime objective and not letting irrelevant shit distract you. You could have left me out there with my pants hanging down," Bonner said.

"I'm sorry. I had the same thought. I didn't mean to make light of it."

"All's well that ends well," Bonner said as Odacio pulled to a stop in front of the nursing home. Kristen started crossing the street.

"I should go. Kristen's getting in." He hung up. She opened the door. He was only twenty minutes late. He could tell already that she wasn't annoyed.

"Hey," she said cheerily as she got in.

"Sorry."

"No problem. Were you at the rally? I figured that was why you were late."

"Kind of. I missed most of it. I tried to break up a fight and got arrested by accident. But they figured it out and let me go quickly. That's why I was late."

"That's as good an excuse as I've heard. It sounded like the rally was big, maybe 700 people," Kristen said.

"Where did you hear that?"

"Sonia Gonzales's Twitter."

"Anything else?" Odacio asked.

"She tweeted something about American Dawn setting up platoons or something. I'm sure she'll have an article up soon enough. Take me home so I can change, but then take me out to dinner."

"Where do you want to go?" Odacio asked.

"I've been dying to go to that place on Wiltshire ever since you mentioned tacos the other night."

15

Chapter 15

Odacio woke up stewing and with a pit in his stomach. The way an introvert might feel right before arriving at a social obligation, only magnified. The die was cast, a crime had already been committed, but yesterday it was Bonner getting his hands dirty. Today they'd be doing the dirty work together.

He thought back to the conversation he had at the taco shop — the one at lunch with Bonner, not the one at dinner with Kristen last night. Bonner was hellbent on doing it alone and didn't want Odacio getting mixed up in it. Maybe it was bluster, but it didn't seem that way. It seemed sincere. It wasn't too late for Odacio to change his mind, he thought to himself. On one hand, it would be easy to back out, but it really didn't feel that way.

Was he worried about what Bonner would think of him if he did back out or try to call it off? Hell, a couple of days ago, that wouldn't have mattered; he didn't even know Bonner. His mind moved to Kristen; this was about her safety. But that didn't work either. She'd be no more or less safe with him there and maybe safer if he stayed with her.

Maybe it was because he couldn't sit with the idea of another man doing the work of keeping his wife safe. Wasn't he adequate? Did she need two husbands or three or just him?

I'm overthinking it, he thought to himself. But he couldn't stop.

He thought about who he was and what this decision said about him, what this meant about his character. Did doing this mean he wasn't the person he always told himself he was? Did backing out mean the same thing?

He looked over and realized that Kristen wasn't there. She had already gotten out of bed. He did too. At the bottom of the stairs, there was a clock, and he realized for the first time that it was 10 a.m., probably later than he'd slept since college. As he headed into the kitchen, he saw Kristen reading the paper, she had already been out to the store, and back he thought. He considered whether that was safe and decided it wasn't. But what's done is done, he thought and didn't want to start the day with an argument, so he decided not to mention it. Instead, he went to the coffee maker and poured himself a cup.

"Good morning."

"Good morning," she said, half distracted, reading an article in the paper.

"What're you reading about?"

"An op-ed about vaccines and anti-vaxxers. This person definitely doesn't like Jenny McCarthy."

"I disagree with that," he said.

"What do you mean?"

"I liked Jenny McCarthy a lot in high school."

"Fuck off. You want to talk about good-looking people?"

"No," Odacio responded quickly.

"Colt Faircloth."

"Who?" Odacio asked.

"Colt Faircloth. He was one of the speakers at the rally yesterday. A big picture is printed of him next to the story. He looks like Blake Shelton."

"Is that guy supposed to be good-looking?"

"Uh, he won the sexiest man alive maybe a year or two ago."

"Whatever. And what's this Colt guy's story?" Odacio asked.

"He was one of the speakers, like the vice president of it or something. He said something about having a platoon leader in every neighborhood by year's end."

"What else did the article say?"

"Not a whole lot. They revised the crowd estimate down to 600, but it was still the largest demonstration ever in Kole. Oh, one other thing, they're doing a letter-writing campaign urging Brody Wilcox to reject whatever deal he's offered and go to trial."

"Wow. That is so easy for them to do from where they're sitting. I've never even heard of something like that," Odacio said.

"That's one of their things, I guess."

"Hey, just a reminder, I'm going fishing with Bonner this afternoon. I'll be back at eight or eight-thirty at the latest," he said. "If I don't get back in time, I'll meet you at Jack and Donna's."

"Okay, but don't people usually go fishing early in the morning?"

"I've never been fishing. I think Bonner knows what he's doing."

"It might get cold. Bring your gloves. Also, I think it's good you're taking my advice on him," she said.

It was 4:55 p.m. Bonner and Odacio were sitting about eight hundred feet away from the Brown's barn, in the woods. They had set up a makeshift table and chairs using a downed tree and a couple of rocks. The receiver and speaker sat on the tree table along with their keys, wallets, and cell phones. The temperature had already dropped, it was unseasonably cold for September, and they were both wearing gloves. They could hear some clanking, like the moving around of chairs, but they hadn't heard any voices yet. They heard something that sounded like a door opening.

"Hey Brian," a voice said.

"Hey, Keith. I'm the first one? I thought there'd be more people here by now."

"Sorry I didn't call you. I changed it to an Executive Committee Meeting. I felt like we had some stuff to sort out among ourselves. I sent a text to all of you yesterday," Keith said.

"I must have missed it. But that sounds right to me. I thought Colt got out ahead of us yesterday."Odacio and Bonner gave each other a thumbs up. The sound was coming through loud and clear.

"Do you know who Brian is?" Odacio asked.

"You think I know everyone in Kole by voice?"

"Guess not," Odacio said.

"Why don't you take a seat, Brian? Get off that leg?" a woman's voice said.

"Getting up and down is harder than just staying up. I'll sit when we get started,"

"Can I get you a beer?" she asked.

"I'm okay, thanks," he responded. After a few minutes, what sounded like two more men arrived. There was some cross-talk coming through on the receiver. Both Bonner and Odacio strained to identify who was saying what. It was all pleasantries, nothing substantive, but they needed to memorize the sound of each voice.

Bonner looked at Odacio and said, "I think I do know the two men who just walked in. It sounded like Lenora called the one Clay and the other Bill. That's gotta be Clay and Bill Thorne. They're brothers. Both served in the first Gulf War. Hard to believe those boys are pushing fifty already, my sister used to babysit the younger one."

"Are they bad guys?" Odacio asked.

"I don't think of them that way," Bonner said.

"What do you make of Keith changing it to an Executive Committee meeting?" Odacio asked.

"If they're plotting something in regards to Kristen, it's more likely we'll hear about it now. And we won't have to wait around for the after-party."

A few minutes passed, and it sounded like either two or three more men had arrived. They listened intently to try to catch names and attach names to voices. It was difficult. They had surmised that the woman was Lenora, and they thought they heard her say, "how's your mother, doing Colt?" He responded, and they determined him to be Colt Faircloth, and his voice was distinct. It was raspy.

"Okay," Odacio turned to Bonner. "It sounds like we've got Faircloth, Keith, Lenora, a guy named Brian, and if you're right, Clay and Bill Thorne. Have you heard any other voices?"

"I think I heard at least one more voice. Maybe two. But I haven't heard an additional name." Bonner said. They continued to listen to a bunch of small talk.

"Dammit," Odacio said. "Get the fucking meeting going; it's

cold."

"I did a stakeout once," Bonner said. "We had good intel that a dealer was going to use his mother's living room as the site of a big buy. I'm talking two hundred and fifty g's. We were after the supplier. We knew it was going down Memorial Day weekend, but we didn't know which day. Four fucking days in a van listening to mindless chatter, Delilah, and God knows what else. I nearly lost my mind."

"Did it work out in the end?"

"Not at all. I don't know if it was bad intel, plans changed, or maybe they purposefully fed us bad information just to bore us to death."

It was 5:25 p.m. when they heard Keith say, "I think we should get started. Stand for the pledge."

Their voices spoke in unison…"I pledge allegiance to the flag of the United States of America and to the republic for which it stands, one nation under God, indivisible with liberty and justice for all."

"I call today's meeting to order. As a reminder, I trust that everyone left their phones in the car as we adopted the no phones policy at the last meeting. May I have a motion to suspend Robert's Rules of Order for this meeting?"

"Motion."

"Second."

"All in favor? The ayes have it. Motion carries. We have a few pieces of business today. I'm just going to name the elephant in the room to get that out of the way. It's the business about the platoons. But I think we put our differences aside for the moment and discuss the Nellie's issue. We know yesterday was a big success, and we don't need to spend time patting ourselves on the back, am I right?"

"Agreed," Colt said.

"Good then," Keith reclaimed the floor. "The Nellie's issue is our opportunity. It confirms everything we've been saying all this time. This is the moment that we go national."

Then a voice that Bonner believed to be Clay Thorne began, "I agree there's an upside, Keith. But we also have to be thinking about the downside of this thing and what we can do to mitigate it. Let's imagine for a moment that if they actually are trying to pin it on us, our standing with the public would take a major hit."

"They can't pin it on us if they can't prove it, and they can't prove it if it didn't happen," Keith responded.

"You know as well as I do that they can prove anything they want. They'll just conjure up the evidence. They're already talking all about a defector. We know that ain't anything." Clay responded.

"I've got the most to lose in that scenario. They'd want to cut off the head, but let's play it out for a second. We'd maintain our innocence. We could probably get the President to tweet for us through Congressman Martindale," Keith said.

"Martindale is important, but I don't think he or any man can control what Trump tweets," Clay said. "I think we need to go on the offensive and clear ourselves of this thing."

"How would we even do that?"

"I think we call a press conference right outside Nellie's. I think we talk about how that place was a positive example of a hard-working black family getting ahead and that whoever did it is a coward. I can say I was just in there over the weekend. Junior and I were there for lunch."

"I wouldn't do that, Clay," a voice they believed to belong to Brian interjected. "Hell, the Feds would think you bombed the place."

"Okay, but the idea still makes sense," Clay said.

"I think you're on to something, but it needs more hashing out," Keith said.

"Gentlemen," Colt began, "I think you're both off the mark. I think you're too wound up thinking about public opinion."

"We need public opinion on our side. It's important," Clay said.

"Why? Do you think we live in a democracy?" Colt retorted. "Because we don't. We know full well it's the cabal. They've got thousands of people throughout the government steering things. Congress is no help neither, even when the Republicans have it. We'll win public opinion in the end by showing strength and being the winners. The public loves a winner."

"And I'm saying we won't win if the public thinks we have blood on our hands. The public has influence." Clay fired back.

"What are you telling me? That no blood is going to spill when the civil war begins? " Colt asked.

Clay raised his voice, causing some distortion on the receiver, "It makes absolutely no sense for us to start a civil war so long as Trump is in the White House!"

"You all make too much of Trump if you ask me," Colt retorted. "You make too much of the presidency. Hell, the man couldn't even repeal Obamacare. You think he can take down the cabal? Hell, Q's account was compromised months ago. Don't you notice more and more the things he says will happen, turn out not to happen?" Colt fired back. "We can't rely on Q anymore, and we can't rely on Trump neither. We need to raise a citizen army, and the longer we wait, the longer we're at a disadvantage."

"We need to bide our time, Colt, and not get ahead of

ourselves," Keith interjected. "The time to raise the citizen army will come; we all agree on that, but not while Trump is in the White House. That's been our position all along."

"But man, don't you see, that position is out of date. Sure that made sense before, but with Q out of the picture, I don't know; I think the time is now," Colt fired back.

"We don't all agree that Q's been compromised, Colt," Clay said. "Some of the evidence you presented was convincing, I'll give you that, but you're jumping to conclusions."

"Q was a great American, but he's dead now. Or in some prison cell somewhere. I don't understand why you can't see that?" Colt said.

Back in the woods, Odacio looked at Bonner and said, "I don't know whether to be terrified or what. This is so fucking weird."

"They really are getting carried away with themselves. Especially that one of them, Colt," Bonner said.

"They're talking about an open insurrection against the United States immediately following the flag pledge for Christ's sake," Odacio said.

The meeting continued round in circles for about fifteen or twenty minutes, with each of them taking turns waxing poetic until a voice they believed belonged to Brian said, "Gentlemen, we're not getting anywhere fast, and I need to meet Leslie at her mother's house by six-thirty. I think what we're really talking about, without talking about it directly, is this issue of the platoons. We need to talk about the platoons because it's the elephant in the room like Keith said. Now, Colt, I must say, you worked the crowd well yesterday, but you went too far on that platoon issue. We hadn't agreed to that internally yet."

"And I do apologize. I really do. I wasn't trying to subvert this body. I just get so worked up sometimes, and at that moment, it just came out," Colt said.

Clay's voice came across the receiver. "I think there are two issues here. There's the issue of the process, which it sounds like we're all in agreement on, but there's also the issue of the substance. I, for one, disagree with the direction the platoon system would take us."

"And why is that?" Colt asked.

"Because I'm uncomfortable with people who aren't part of this deliberative body operating in our name. I'll give you an example right now. Who was that SS362 on the internet suggesting that we would do something with that FBI agent's wife? That crossed a line for me," Clay said.

In the woods, Bonner and Odacio looked at one another as if to say 'bingo' simultaneously. In the barn, Brian responded. "We're on the same page about that, Clay, but in fairness, isn't SS362 the handle Shultz uses? He's harmless. Eight-five years old, he wouldn't go anywhere besides his bed and the bathroom if not occasionally to that library to get on the computer."

"It doesn't matter," Clay said, "It's still not right, and that's not the right look for American Dawn."

"Gentlemen, what do they say?" Colt began. "We need to let a thousand flowers bloom. To get thousands of beautiful flowers, we're going to need to tolerate some ugly ones."

"We need discipline and order, Colt," Keith responded. "No organization runs well without discipline and order!"

"No. That's where your thinking is wrong, Keith, respectfully. You're sitting here thinking about how to run an organization, and we need our minds wrapped around how to launch a movement."

"We've been over this before, Colt!" Clay said. "We've gotta run American Dawn as best as we can to *support* the movement. We can't *be* the movement."

"Hear me out. We talked about what would happen when the civil war breaks out. Part of the military is going get behind us, but part isn't. We know we're likely to lose the first round. Then it's going to be us against the depleted military, but we're still going to be outgunned, right? And what do we know about the only way to beat an army when you're outgunned?" Colt paused for a few seconds and then continued, "guerilla warfare, gentlemen. And in order to have effective guerilla warfare, you need autonomy and decentralization. Sure, we need to deliver the command intent centrally, but the organization has to be decentralized."

For the first time, they heard Lenora chime in. "Well, I think Colt is right. The first sensemaking thing I heard in a while was when he started talking about setting up the platoon leaders in all the neighborhoods. We need a strategy that can actually win in the end, or else we're just here spinning our wheels and listening to each other talk."

"Lenora, I will remind you that you are not on this Executive Committee. We appreciate your company, but I must ask you to refrain from engaging in a matter like this," Keith said.

"What are you afraid of, Keith?" Colt said. "Is it control? Is it power? What is it? You can have a lot of control over this small thing here, or you can have some control over something massive and effective. Which is it going to be?"

"This is about effectiveness, Colt!" Keith yelled causing distortion, "If I thought the thing you were saying would work, I might support it, but I think it will fall flat! It will fail!"

"Well, at least we fail then trying to win, trying to run a strategy that can actually accomplish our mission," Colt retorted.

"Gentlemen," Brian interjected. "I think we know the arguments. We should bring the question to the membership and take a vote. We're not breaking new ground here, and I've got to get to Leslie's mother's house." Everyone seemed to agree. The Executive Committee members mulled about for a bit, saying their goodbyes.

Back in the woods, Bonner and Odacio started to debrief. "What do you think?" Odacio asked.

"I think you should take precautions, but it doesn't seem Kristen is in any real danger."

"Yeah, that's clear. What about the rest of it?"

"I think they're one step off some sort of role-playing game, like my nephew's playing dungeons and dragons when they were kids," Bonner said.

"You don't find that Colt guy problematic?"

"Colt? Yeah. We oughta lock him up before he does something nuts, but the rest of them are fine if you ask me," Bonner said.

"I want to listen to the tape again."

"You can listen to it all you want," Bonner said as he lit a cigarette. As he did, their attention was drawn back to the barn. It sounded like a fight was brewing. By the time Bonner and Odacio made sense of what was going on, Keith and Lenora were in full screaming match mode. It was hard to hear exactly what they were saying, but Keith was obviously mad about Lenora taking Colt's side. They heard Lenora cry out in pain.

Odacio's fist was clenched and shaking. Bonner noticed. "Calm down, kid. This ain't our business." It was escalating fast. "Odacio, look at me! We ain't here for this!" Bonner screamed

135

but under his breath. At this point, Bonner and Odacio heard the sounds of violence. "Look at me, Odacio. I'm shutting off the receiver! Don't fucking think about it." But it was too late. Bonner leaped to tackle Odacio and got his hands around his waist. Odacio was in full stride dragging him behind, and eventually, Bonner had to let go. By the time Bonner got to his feet again, Odacio was easily 200 feet ahead.

When Odacio burst through the barn door, Keith had one hand around Lenora's neck and another clutching a fistful of her hair. Odacio scared the shit out of both of them with his entrance, and Keith threw Lenora headfirst into the concrete support beam that held up the barn. She dropped face down before Odacio even processed what had happened. With Keith stunned, Odacio rushed towards Lenora and turned her over. She wasn't conscious. A total of like five seconds had passed since he stormed in. He was on his knees. Two more seconds passed. He felt something wrong and looked up. Keith Brown had a gun pointed at his head. Odacio didn't have his piece on him. Big mistake. Brown had rage in his eyes, but with no time for words to come out, another crash was heard when the barn door flew open again. Seconds felt like minutes. Time had slowed to a crawl for Odacio, every little twitch visible and registering. Brown was scared shitless; Odacio could see it. Bonner was in the doorway, and Keith's gun was moving in that direction. Odacio saw the index finger move ever so slightly. He registered Brown's eyes weren't on him, and so he lunged for the gun but got the wrist, his momentum forcing Brown's hand and the gun upwards. One shot fired. It was loud, so loud all Odacio heard was ringing. He felt like he just came-to from a knockout. He looked down at Keith Brown's face, but it wasn't there. It was gone.

Odacio was in a daze like an out-of-body experience, but Bonner was in a rage. By the time Odacio realized what was going on, Bonner had his left hand around Odacio's neck, pushing him against the wall and whaling on him with his other hand. Odacio realized he wasn't getting punched, he was getting slapped hard, and it hurt. But he put forward no defense. Bonner ran out of steam or decided to stop. The ringing in Odacio's left ear was different now from the ringing in his right ear. It was worse. That's where Bonner was hitting him. He looked at Bonner, who was now hunched over with his hands on his knees and looking at the ground. He sounded guttural. "What did you do, kid? What did you do?"

Odacio thought about the question for a second. His back slowly slid down the barn wall until his ass reached the floor, his knees up. Head lowered onto his knees, with his hands resting crossways blocking out the light, he was one step removed from the fetal position. He began to cry hard, but it didn't last long. He looked over at Lenora and transformed back into an FBI agent almost instantaneously. He crawl-ran over to her. Lenora's eyes were open, but she was nonresponsive. She was dead too. He fell backward onto his butt, balancing himself upright with his palms on the barn floor. He didn't know how much time passed before he felt Bonner grabbing him by the collar pulling him up to his feet.

"We're leaving," Bonner said.

"What?"

"We're leaving."

"What are we doing?"

"We're leaving. This was a murder-suicide. That's what it looks like; that's what it will be," Bonner said.

"We need to call this in," Odacio said.

"Alright, call it in," Bonner said, waiting with his hands on his hips. Odacio reached into his pockets, looking for his phone. "The phones are back at those rocks. We'll talk about it on the way," Bonner said, giving Odacio a push as they walked towards the door. Bonner considered locking the door behind them on the way out but decided not to. He closed the door behind them as they walked out. They headed back to the rock formation, walking slowly. The distance to the rocks was almost three football fields long. Odacio was regaining his wits and composure, finally able to think straight, or as straight as one could in a moment like this.

"I've got to call this in, Bonner."

"If you've gotta, you gotta," Bonner said. "What are you going to tell them my role was? Just so I know."

"I think you should leave," Odacio said. "I was here alone."

"How did you get here? What are you going to tell them about the bug?"

"I don't know, I got dropped off and that I had the bug from an old case."

"They'll trace it back to my office," Bonner said. "There's also an issue with Kristen. If I hadn't driven by your house to pick you up, a bad idea of mine in retrospect, it could have been that you lied to her, but not now. We're here together."

"I'm sure we can come up with something," Odacio said. "Let's just think for a minute."

"I can call it in myself."

"Forget it," Odacio said.

"It was my idea."

"But it was my fault. I went in," Odacio said.

"What's the sense in both of us doing time for manslaughter? One of us should take the rap."

"Yeah. Me," Odacio said.

"Is that what Kristen would want?"

"I think so," Odacio said.

"First, you ain't thinking straight. Second, you know nothing," Bonner said as he started to pretend he was talking to her. "Hello Kristen, should your husband go to jail for accidentally killing a man who was beating his wife, or do you prefer that not happen?"

"It's more complicated than that, and it could be that neither of us does time."

"That's a chance we can take. But do you think Kristen should have a say in it?"

"What are we going to do, call her up?" Odacio asked.

"What we do next is the most important decision you'll ever make. Do you want to make it alone, or do you want to make it with her?"

"If I call her, it brings her into it."

"If you call her and she says we should report it, then it makes no difference because she would know tonight anyway," Bonner said.

"But if she tells me not to, then I've brought her into a cover-up."

"Yeah, so we have three options. Call it in without telling her, cover it up without telling her, or tell her the situation, and the two of you make the decision together."

"When you put it that way, it feels like I should call her."

"I'll follow your lead on this," Bonner said.

"I don't know what I'm going to say."

"Come to think of it; we shouldn't call her. If we decide to cover it up, we don't want a record of the call from here. We could go talk to her about it together. If she says to call it in, we drive back here and call it in," Bonner said.

"She's at our neighbors' house. She told me she was going over early since I wasn't having dinner with her."

"Well, let's go get her out of there."

16

Chapter 16

They were fast approaching Jack and Donna's house without a plan for how to extract Kristen. "Ok, how about this?" Bonner said. "We pull up, and I pop the hood. You go to the door and ring the bell. Tell them I was dropping you off on the way to my mother's. I'm having car trouble. You're gonna drive me, but it's like a two-hour drive, and you want Kristen to come with you. Take a rain check on the social visit."

"That's not bad; that should work," Odacio said. They pulled up in front of the house. It was a nice well kept suburban home with a large front yard. The covered porch was lit up and welcoming. It looked like a scene from fifties television.

The house was set back about fifty yards from the road. Bonner popped the hood, stepped out, and stood in front of the car as if he was doing something. Odacio ran up through the yard and rang the bell. Bonner saw Kristen and the wife greet Odacio at the door. There was a lot of hand talking and muffled voices. Odacio pointed at Bonner, the two women waved, and Bonner waved back. More hand talking. It was taking longer than Bonner expected. Kristen was looking at Bonner now, beckoning him. "Come on up, Brett!" she yelled.

"What the fuck?" he said to himself. Kristen repeated herself, and he started walking up towards the door. As he approached the porch, they were all smiles. He was trying to make sense of what was happening.

"Brett, this is Donna, and Donna, this is Brett!" Kristen said. Odacio was standing there like a deer in the headlights.

"Pleasure to meet you, ma'am."

"Of course! Call me Donna."

"When we go inside, we'll introduce you to Jack!"

"Inside?" Bonner asked.

"Yup. Follow me!" Donna said, turning and marching in with Kristen behind her. Bonner turned to Odacio.

"What the fuck is going on?" he asked under his breath.

"The story didn't work," Odacio said.

"What do you mean? Shit. Forget about it. What are we doing?" Bonner asked.

"We need to go inside. When I mentioned your mother, Kristen kind of took over the conversation, she wanted to know all about her."

"My mother died during childbirth!" Bonner yelled under his breath.

"That explains a lot. Fuck. Why did you tell me to say that then? Why not say we're visiting your father?" Odacio responded, annoyed.

"Because he died years ago," Bonner snapped back.

"This was a stupid cover story!"

"From what I remember, you didn't have a better idea!"

"Come on, you two!" they heard Kristen calling from inside.

"Let's just do what we've got to do and get out of here fast,"

Bonner said.

They walked into the living room. Donna and Kristen were sitting at the table. Jack walked in with a platter of those little hot dog thingies. "Jack, this is Brett Bonner, Brett this is Jack."

"Nice to meet you," Jack said.

"You as well," Bonner replied.

"Brett, my father was an auto mechanic, and he forced me to learn the trade. I never used it for work, but I know a thing or two. Let me take a look at your car," Jack said.

"Oh no. I couldn't."

"It's no bother at all. It'll be fun," Jack said.

"No, it's not that," Bonner said.

"I insist."

"Well, you see, a good friend of mine is a mechanic downtown, and if I didn't give him the work, you know, I'd just feel bad about it."

"Wait a minute, you mean Jake, from Jake's Autobody? I used to go with his daughter before I met Donna. In fact, I'm probably going to see him this week," Jack said.

"No. A different one."

"I think he's the only one downtown," Jack said.

"It's a private garage. Word of mouth clientele only, that sort of thing. I'd get you in, but there's a three-year waiting list."

"For an auto mechanic? He must be out of this world," Jack said.

Kristen interjected, helpfully getting him out of that situation, "Come sit down." Bonner and Odacio did what she said. "I know you need to go to your mother's, but we promised Jack and Donna we'd play just one game."

"Okay... what are we playing?" Bonner asked. Donna reached under the table and pulled out a box.

"Monopoly!" she said with a big smile.

"Whoa, wait a minute now. That game takes three hours. My momma's waiting."

"It's not a problem at all," Kristen said. "We play a faster version where you deal out all the properties randomly at the beginning and start by trading."

"Won't it still be a long game?"

"It'll be over before you know it. You've got to tell me about your mother. What kind of woman is she?" Kristen asked.

Bonner paused and looked at Odacio, but he was no help. "Old. She is an old woman."

"Well, of course, she's an old woman, but what was she like when you were just a boy?"

"Uh, she was strict, like a lot of mothers were back then."

"Tell us a story. A memory."

Bonner paused and thought for a few long seconds, initially drawing a blank. "Okay. This one time, I was supposed to paint the fence. I tricked all the neighborhood kids into doing it for me. Well, she caught wind of it, and boy was she mad." Odacio looked at him disapprovingly; the air was thick with awkwardness.

Kristen broke the silence. "Um. Brett. That's not a memory. That's from Tom Sawyer by Mark Twain."

Bonner took a breath. "I'm sorry. It's just that she's taken ill, and I don't really want to discuss it too much."

"Good save, Bonner," Odacio thought to himself.

"We all put up a tough exterior, Brett," Kristen began. "But under that shell, we all have the same feelings."

Bonner stepped away from the table as they dealt out the cards to call Triple-A. He had them come tow his car to back up their story. Odacio and Bonner tried to move the game along as quickly as they could. They were making moves that were akin to taking dives but trying to do so just subtly enough that they looked like bad Monopoly players, not two guys who were purposefully trying to lose fast.

The game ended about forty minutes later, and everyone said their goodbyes. The three of them walked out. Kristen was parked on the road. The three of them got in the car, and when all of their doors closed, it was immediately apparent that Kristen was furious. "What the fuck was that in there?" she started. "First you!" she said, looking at Odacio, "Trading Marvin Gardens for Baltic, that's fucking ridiculous! And you," looking to Bonner, "trading away the railroad monopoly for St James and Tennessee? You know, Bonner, I have half a mind to ask if you even have a mother!"

"You're right. We've got to talk," Odacio said.

They recounted everything to Kristen back at the Odacios' and framed the choice to her. She was sitting with both of them on the back porch, staring out at the stars. It was a clear, beautiful night.

"Before I answer," she began, "I just want to repeat back what I'm hearing so you can confirm that I understand correctly."

"Okay," Odacio said.

"A geriatric man who uses the library to get on the internet made a vague threat about me. In response, the two of you decided to plant an illegal wiretap. The people you wiretapped want to start a civil war but can't agree on how or when and have no actual plans to do so, nor any plans or designs on me. You went to their house and killed their leader, his wife is dead too, and their bodies are in their barn. Did I miss anything?"

"Kristen, you say it like that, but hindsight is 20-20! And you left out the part that killing the guy was an accident and may have saved Bonner's life!" Odacio said.

"Yeah, Kristen, it all happened really fast," Bonner said.

Odacio's phone rang. He looked at the screen. "It's Jackie. Why's he calling so late on a Saturday?"

"Answer it, but get off quickly," Kristen said.

"Good evening, sir," he said and then paused to listen. "No problem." He paused again and listened to Jackie for about half a minute.

"Well, I appreciate the call, sir. You have a good night." Odacio hung up.

"What was that?" Bonner asked.

"He didn't want to wait until Monday to tell me that they determined the threat against Kristen was not credible."

"Too bad American Dawn doesn't meet on Sundays," Bonner said.

"Let's get back to it," Kristen said. "The question for me comes down to the odds. Why do you think you'd get away with it?"

Bonner answered, "They're known to be violent with one another, and he did shoot himself in the face. It looks like a murder-suicide. It's not an uncommon occurrence. The boys at the meeting will say the Browns were alone when they left. Odacio and I were wearing gloves. No prints. When the bodies get discovered, it will be my crime scene and my investigation. I'll steer it right where it needs to go."

"That actually sounds pretty airtight," Kristen said.

"Nothing is airtight, Kristen," Odacio said. "Believe me, the events of the past two days really demonstrate that."

"Yeah. I know, but if there were ever an instance where someone could get away with murder, this seems like it. And people do get away with murder."

"They definitely do," Bonner said.

"I don't feel good about this," Odacio said.

"I feel fine about it," Kristen said. "Well, wait, that's an overstatement. This is something I can live with. I don't care that Keith Brown is dead. I don't wish him dead, but if he hadn't attacked his wife, he'd still be alive. That's the bottom line."

"Are you sure? I'm afraid you're never going to look at me the same again," Odacio said.

"Well, it isn't the kind of thing one just forgets ever happened, but if you gave up your career and did time for something like this when you have a choice in the matter…I just don't see it as a rational choice."

"It's settled then," Bonner said. "We'll discover the bodies when we execute the warrant for those computers on Monday."

Maybe they will or maybe they won't. But you'll have to join us next time to find out, on…the Frontline.

17

Next Time...

J oin us next time as Odacio and Bonner race to cover up one crime and solve another, on Episode 2 of The Frontline.

If you enjoyed Episode 1, You can get the next episode, or better yet, get the entire season at a discount. Also, please consider leaving a review. It makes a big difference for an author like me who's just starting out.

If you have questions or would like more information, you can reach me by emailing michaelsantino@protonmail.com or visiting kolecounty.com.

Thanks to Delis and Liz for many hours of editing (and Liz for cover work). Thanks to Brenna McDuffie for the editorial assessment. And thanks to Alex and Joe for some free legal advice that helped make the story more true to life.